CW01184699

Water:
A Chronicle

Nguyễn Ngọc Tư, a talented and highly acclaimed female writer of the Vietnam Writers Association (Hội Nhà Văn Việt Nam), was born in 1976. With passion, she writes tirelessly and diligently, choosing the most familiar and endearing subjects from her life as basis for her stories, with a quintessentially Southern tonality that has become a signature of her writing. Her short story collection *Cánh đồng bất tận* (*Endless Field*) has received numerous awards, including the LiBeraturpreis Prize 2018, and has been adapted for the stage and screen. Other works of her have earned her the 2018 ASEAN Literature Award, and the 2024 Outstanding Southeast Asian Literature Award by the Dianchi Literature Prize. She was listed by *Forbes* magazine as one of the Top 50 most influential women in Vietnam of 2018. Nguyễn Ngọc Tư's works have been reprinted many times and translated into Korean, English, Swedish, and German.

Nguyễn An Lý lives in Hồ Chí Minh City. Her translations into Vietnamese include works by Margaret Atwood, Kazuo Ishiguro, J. L. Borges, Amos Oz, and the poetry in *The Lord of the Rings*. She won English PEN Translates Awards for *Chinatown* (Tilted Axis Press, 2022) and *Elevator in Sài Gòn* (Tilted Axis Press, 2024) by Thuận, and *Water: A Chronicle* (Major Books, 2024) by Nguyễn Ngọc Tư. *Chinatown* also won the 2023 ALTA National Translation Award in Prose and was the runner-up of the 2023 TA First Translation Prize. She co-founds and co-edits the independent online *Zzz Review*.

MAJOR BOOKS

Major Books is an independent press dedicated to bringing Vietnamese literature to the English-speaking world. Our name speaks as a clear, bold, and audacious resistance against the 'minor' status attributed to certain languages and their literature in the global publishing scene. Ranging from critically acclaimed post-war fiction, national epic poetry, to contemporary LGBTQIA+ writings, we hope to present a well-rounded portrait of Vietnam and our diverse voices. Our hope is to contribute, no matter how little, to growing awareness that there are no 'lesser' voices in world literature.

praise

'A tap is left running, and nothing will stop the flow and the flooding until the woman who turned it on comes back. But who is she, exactly, and how in the whole wide world can she be tracked and found? At once mythical and ultra-modern, this is a compelling story of the strange fluidities and tenacities of human identity and behaviour in the media-saturated environments of the twenty-first century, as ever.'—Rachel Bowlby FBA, Professor of Comparative Literature, University College London

'A flowing, surreal tableaux, this book lends mythic quality to its many characters washing up on the shores of readers' imagination. A woman literally seeks a cult leader's heart to cure her baby, and traverses a river to do so—but who is she, really? Nguyễn Ngọc Tư opens so many doors of possibility, laid out in Nguyễn An Lý's playfully acerbic translation. One inhabitant of these stories says, "I could feast my eyes on them as the boat passed further into a world afloat", and such is the reader speaking of so many you will meet in this author's fascinating vision. This is a grimey, watery tale of the always-unexpected, of rough surrounds lending themselves to all kinds of fervor.'—Khairani Barokka, author of *amuk*

'*Water: A Chronicle* is a triumph of lyrical storytelling that explores the Mekong Delta as a mythical place haunted by loss and longing. Through vivid sensory details, Nguyễn Ngọc Tư expertly evokes the emotions of characters embarking on journeys of bodily and spiritual transformation. The ghostly atmosphere of the setting enchanted me, and I couldn't put the book down until I reached the end.'—Nghiem Tran, author of *We're Safe When We're Alone*

'An existential querie'—*Người Lao Động* press

'... the measly 125 pages somehow still manage to make us feel the immense efforts of the author in building layers of sounds and meanings in such few words—*Tuổi Trẻ* press

'... since lives are always land-bound, in *Water: A Chronicle* this land is the submerged delta, where the same water that raises us up is also the one that sinks us down to the bottom...'—*Trạm Đọc* press

'... when a book is so good that one forgets to sleep, forgets to eat reading, then the eight-year wait is truly worth it.'—*Phụ Nữ* press

'Parallel hells'—*Bookish*

'Studying Nguyễn Ngọc Tư's novel by narratology, the narrator is one of the important problems that show her renovation in creation method.'—Trần Minh Thư and Bùi Thanh Thảo from Cần Thơ University

'... human's fate in the shape of water'—*Literature* press

'... a tsunami that once opened, cannot be closed'—*Art Times* press

Major Books Ltd, 128 City Road, London, United Kingdom, EC1V 2NX
First published in the United Kingdom in 2024 by Major Books

Copyright © 2020 Nguyễn Ngọc Tư
Originally published in Vietnamese as *Biên Sử Nước*
by Phụ Nữ Publishing House and distributed by Phanbook
English translation © 2024 Nguyễn An Lý
Cover art © 2024 Nguyễn Thanh Vũ

Edited by Deborah Smith

Nguyễn Ngọc Tư has asserted her moral right under the Copyright, Designs and Patents Act, 1988, to be identified as the author of this work.

The moral right of Nguyễn An Lý to be identified as the translator of this work has been asserted in accordance with the Copyright, Designs and Patents Act 1988

All Rights Reserved.
No part of this publication may be copied, reproduced, leased, licensed, transmitted, or publicly performed in any form or by any means, electronic or mechanical, including photocopy, recording or any other information storage and retrieval system, without prior permission in writing from Major Books.

A CIP catalogue record for this book is available from the British Library
ISBN 978-1-917233-00-2
eISBN 978-1-917233-01-9

Typeset in Garamond Premier Pro by Coral Books JSC
Printed and bound in Vietnam by Hai Phong Stationery and Packaging Company
www.major-books.com

ENGLISH PEN
FREEDOM TO **WRITE**
FREEDOM TO **READ**

This book has been selected to receive financial
assistance from English PEN's PEN Translates programme,
supported by Arts Council England. English PEN exists to promote
literature and our understanding of it, to uphold writers'
freedoms around the world, to campaign against the persecution
and imprisonment of writers for stating their views,
and to promote the friendly co-operation of writers
and the free exchange of ideas.

www.englishpen.org

Supported using public funding by
ARTS COUNCIL ENGLAND

Water:
A Chronicle

Nguyễn Ngọc Tư

Translated by Nguyễn An Lý

contents

praise 5

a word from the publisher 14

chapter one

to the river she's arrived 23

chapter two

sighs that taste of salt 24

chapter three

the mark of water 30

chapter four

calling aloud 52

chapter five
water rising 64

chapter six
cocoons 84

chapter seven
a cry from the sky 100

chapter eight
the shadow bride 116

chapter nine
fairy ascending 130

chapter ten
no one comes wake up 145

chapter eleven
leaving 153

translator's note 155

a word from the publisher

Water: A Chronicle (henceforth *Water*) is a novel of perpetual seeking. The story opens with a woman carrying a child, who embarks on an endless quest for the heart that will cure all ailments. Along the vast river, various characters seek this woman—whether as a mother, a daughter, or a neighbour, each hoping she holds the key to their own quest. Meanwhile, street gangs, in their reverence and servitude to the Lord, pursue salvation, riches, and prosperity. All in vain.

The Vietnamese mother with her child, toiling across terrains in search of the human heart, is the lynchpin of all stories—of the society depicted by Nguyễn Ngọc Tư. She is the heart of the Delta, the source of the narrative stream, intertwining the motivations of every character and driving the core of the intrigue. Despite existing as a mere whisper or shadow, the women Nguyễn Ngọc Tư writes are far from passive objects. In *Water*, they may not speak, but they are not silenced. Even if they are not the active cause of calamity, they loom beyond the riverbank like a monstrous threat.

Who is this female figure? It is revealed that there is not just one seeking mother, but many, each distinct yet united by a shared resolve. Yet, despite their multiplicity, they remain elusive, always just out of reach. What motivates these women to leave everything behind and pursue a journey to an island that might not exist? To a cure that inevitably proves to be a con?

What is it that, in turn, Nguyễn Ngọc Tư seeks? Certainly not a straightforward answer. Like the overflowing fables that spring from the narrative tap that is a woman with child, Nguyễn Ngọc Tư seeks to keep on telling stories. Stories about people from a land, real or imagined, that deserve to be told.

Hailing from Cà Mau, Vietnam's southernmost province, Nguyễn Ngọc Tư caught Vietnam's attention with her debut collection *Ngọn Đèn Không Tắt* (*The Inextinguishable Light*), which earned the top prize of the Hồ Chí Minh City's Writers Association recognising outstanding literary talent in young writers. She has since garnered widespread acclaim from the Vietnamese literary scene, solidifying herself as a leader in contemporary Vietnamese writing.

With a distinct dialect evocative of the Mekong Delta, she often refuses to clarify on local particularities, occasionally perplexing even Vietnamese readers. To some, her pen may seem crude, too realistic, too cutting— painfully evocative of the reality from which she draws.

Nguyễn Ngọc Tư herself has recognised this, comparing her writing to a durian. Some savour its taste; others recoil from the fruit's pungent aroma. But the heart of the fruit is encased in a thick, spiky skin that must be hacked into to access. Like the durian, Nguyễn Ngọc Tư's writing does not bend to please anyone. And as an avid follower of Nguyễn Ngọc Tư's work, Nguyễn An Lý's refusal to compromise when translating Vietnamese makes her a well-suited match for the author.

Despite her uncompromising approach, Nguyễn Ngọc Tư's writing is far from inaccessible. Readers across Germany, Sweden, France, China, and Korea enthusiastically received the translations of *Cánh Đồng Bất Tận* (*Endless Field*). Her commercial success in Vietnam, on the other hand, attests to the power of her prose to bridge regional and cultural differences.

While many of her settings derive from remote barges, marginal communities and isolated settlements, there is something universal in her watery landscape. Far from just representing life in a scape where the river rules over all, *Water* explores faith, lawlessness, desperation, and the inner struggles of modern individuals faced with strife and hopelessness. Her images will speak to the reader in the myriads of ways water seeps in every corner of life.

There is also a deeper necessity in translating Nguyễn Ngọc Tư and works of a similar nature. This commitment goes beyond showcasing a dynamic writer's talent and a masterful act of translation. It is also an essential step to diversify whose stories get translated and recognised as part of a global—not national—literary heritage.

Regional disparities exist in Vietnam, as they do everywhere else. The Vietnamese literary canon has long been dominated by Northern, male voices. That is yet another reason to celebrate Nguyễn Ngọc Tư's wide reception and success. Translating her work not only contributes to a global understanding of Vietnam, but also directly challenges conceptions of Vietnam and 'Vietnameseness'. Have voices from Vietnam's Mekong Delta ever been showcased in such a complex light, in narratives centring women, no less? Faced with the stereotype of a rural Vietnam populated by grass, water buffalos, and simple people with earnest hearts, we should question how these frames limit our response to the stories being told.

In reading *Water*, there could be a temptation to see it as representative of rural Vietnam, or of the region from which the author hails. *Water*, while written by a Vietnamese author, is set in a dreamscape, devoid of any real, identifiable locations. Who is to say it represents anything but itself? This is a fine balancing act between holding the importance of Vietnamese representation and refusing to typecast what is 'Vietnam' or 'Vietnamese'.

More than ever, it is important to deepen encounters of this Vietnam beyond news headlines and photo reportages, to come close to understanding how having the water so close, seeping into skin, shapes one's life. For Nguyễn Ngọc Tư's characters, how are they defined beyond their identities shaped by water?

It is thus our honour to work with Nguyễn Ngọc Tư and Nguyễn An Lý to bring her newest novel, brimming with her singular talent, to an English-speaking audience. Mesmerising, poignant, lyrical, and existential, yet claustrophobic, this work truly encapsulates the beauty of what contemporary Vietnamese writing has to offer. It represents what we wish to promote and platform— to challenge the conception of a 'minor' literature, language, or culture. To let stories, in their fullest forms, be faithfully and carefully told and enjoyed, no matter the question of distance, border or language.

We at Major Books hope that you will welcome Nguyễn Ngọc Tư and enjoy her work with the same enthusiasm her readers have shown for the past twenty years.

Major Books
London, 16 September 2024

Those who fall off don't return.

Li-Young Lee

CHAPTER ONE

to the river she's arrived

Day two thousand and forty-six, The Lord has nothing left but his heart. The woman who is to take it has arrived at the river, her babe in her arms.

CHAPTER TWO

sighs that taste of salt

Nothing is left out there. Water has occupied the temple yard, water and darkness. Darkness so thick it has burrowed into the sloppy mud beneath the water. The hard crust has been stripped away. They used to keep an embankment of sorts to keep the river away from plots of land they were gouging, but now it is just water, water everywhere. That was after they had prised out every single brick, gathered every pinch of dust left from the pair of concrete dragons, the stone censer, the stone lamp pillars. From the same yard where they used to prostrate themselves, they prised out everything they could, kissed each item with sobbing reverence, bowed before them, sought to bring them home put them on altars worship them as sacred. Someone broke their collar bone fighting over a fragment of root from the frangipani tree. How many times a day do they burn incense on the altar before that root, I wonder? How many altars will simultaneously light up on that day of my ascension?

Can remember the last blooming still. A riot of white on those gnarly black barren branches. Watching them, not out of any special fondness, but from this throne looking out to the temple yard, the hundred-year-old frangipani tree was the only thing to see. Must have been there even before the isle's first inhabitants. Fat petals on flowers identical in size as if they came from the same mould. Only when they fall can you tell that they are not fake. Fragrance too can be faked. Those women who came on duty at the Upper Chamber, they would startle and look around them on their first day, searching for the laurel plant. 'I can hear its smell so close,' they said. Then, to their embarrassment, they would realise that the honest smell came from the pair of aroma lamps in the corners of the chamber.

White. The colour of those petals. And opaque, their skin was. Flesh hoarding rice water. Striking against the red silk spread. You rubbed and rubbed, but that skin and flesh would not become transparent. Even when it got so damp and sticky, as if they were about to dissolve into water, if you just scraped that salty, gritty sweat away, the skin would seem to have grown more opaque. And white. Like those flowers.

Can still hear them now, at times, the sounds of them pouring water onto themselves. An illusion, Báo says. Just like the sounds of dogs barking, slippered feet squeaking out there in the hallway, patrolmen coughing, crowds jostling for the front spots in the night-drenched yard. They want to be able to see me clearly. 'It's the wind,' Báo says. But, oddly, the wind cannot be heard. In this stripped-bare isle, it is hard to tell that such a thing as the wind exists. No iron sheet with loose nails for it to rattle and bang, no clothes on a drying pole for it to manipulate, no blades of grass to be crushed to the ground. They have taken everything, but everything. If Báo is right and the wind does exist, it is a formless, traceless wind.

Báo cannot be trusted. He brushes off the fact that recently the sighs have been gathering more and more, agitating, clamouring. 'Ghosts are ridiculous enough, sighs my arse,' he said, jerking his chin at the darkness flooding all the way to the river. But the sounds torment ME nightly. A forest of sighs. An ocean of sighs. Dry as sandpaper. Harsh as a curse. Am hungry for human conversation. Any morsel will do, profanity, inanity, aimless greetings. Or the painful screams of those thieving types being whipped in the front yard. The strings of obscenities pouring forth from those blood-salted criminal lips, periodically broken by the air-splitting sounds of ray-tail whip strikes, and the hair-raisingly calm voice of Báo: 'The smallest clod in the Lone Isle belongs to the Lord. How dare you?'

I would be dozing on MY throne, or tumbling in the depths with milk-hoarding skin and flesh. The gold was meticulously watched over by Báo. From the lamps out in the yard, light reached in through the chamber door, inlays of light on the smalls of backs. Even without those lamps, the isle used to have light. The gold gave light to it. That light had stopped us sleeping, those early nights when gold first manifested out in the fields. You closed your eyes and still you saw the blaze.

They took the light away. They took the gold away. Darkness has inhaled the isle into its bottomless bowels. Even the sighs (growing harsher by the day) are dark. It has been some time since the last rain. The sound of rain ought to be more soothing than these sighs. The rattling and banging of thunder is more soothing than these sighs.

'Cô Long is coming back soon,' Báo says, flickering away an imaginary cigarette butt. His supply was exhausted a long time ago. He is visibly excited. An unusual thing. Can't remember who Cô Long is. But the name calls up a hazy taste of salt in the navel. Such a familiar taste, that salt. And those navels. Can remember the taste, but none of the names, they have all blended into one another, and the greater the attempt to think is the harder the sighs soak up all the surrounding air.

Still want air somehow. Why a heart alone would need it. Life without breathing is the only kind that lasts a thousand years. A thousand years from now, will they still be bowing before me? Can't remember the face of him who carried away the lungs. But hard to forget the old man who sought MY eyes. He had bowed so low his forehead struck his prosthetic leg, sobbing, his three cycles of incarnation could not pay back this immense debt. When Báo wrapped up the eyeballs and brought them to him, the old git pissed himself and fainted. He lay there all crumpled while the wind played with the hem of his shirt, revealing a burn mark the size of a hand.

He had come too late. There was nothing left to be bestowed. The gold had long since run out. The latecomers could not find anything, neither the root of a plant nor a handful of dirt. Then a seeker, kissing the ground with his head, asked for a few of those fingernails that had been grown so long they had curled in on themselves. That person reminded ME that this flesh body is also a gift, a gift worthy of the highest adoration.

'It's said that God's body ain't in His tomb,' Báo says. Whenever he says what I am thinking, his eyes flare up. Can't help but suspect that there are knives in them. What will he do with those hidden knives? It has been ages, why is there no hint of rust dimming their shine? A thousand years later, would he still bow before me, with those eye blades?

CHAPTER THREE

the mark of water

I spent the whole evening on my uncle's porch, watching the advance of the night. From the edge of the mango grove, a bat sliced across the dusky yard. My uncle poured the used-up tea leaves into the bed of malnourished garlic chives and wondered aloud if he could find strings for the four corners of the mosquito net. The last time I'd visited Yên Xuyên, I also spent the night here, at mum's younger brother's.

When mum died, her vacated half of the marital bed was filled in the blink of an eye. One would think they'd been waiting for it. Last year, when I came back to remove myself from the family registry, the new woman was in confinement, and the quicklime still looked fresh on mum's tomb in the garden. This afternoon, the baby could already tell strangers from family, shrieking and howling while I rummaged in the altar cabinet for old photos, but mum's tomb was still glaring white.

'Also a Phúc, that one,' my uncle said.

Another bat swung by. Or perhaps the same one, but I couldn't tell. Perhaps only other bats could. My aunt, fresh from her shower, her remaining lock of hair a wet coil upon her crown, spoke into the smoke of the incense she was lighting: 'So many Phúcs in this land, when they reported on the one hunting for a human heart for a cure, I thought...' I knew I had a place inside that ellipsis. Phúc is my name too, same as that of the woman my newspaper bosses were driving themselves crazy over. Who had ended the glory of that isle, extinguishing an entire empire, by taking the heart of its founder.

'Our Yên Xuyên in the spotlight again.' My uncle gave a bitter laugh, handing me a list sent down from the town committee. A list of all the Phúcs, with details copied from the town's family registration ledgers. My uncle disapproved of my quest to learn as much as I could about the woman. What was so special about it; any mother would move heaven and earth for their sick child. They would knock at any door, follow any lead, hunt down any purported healer who might have just the cure for this particular ill. 'It's the 21st century now, you should be shaking people out of their mystification, not adding to it.'

'It'd be a sad world without mystification, uncle.' I held the picture towards the door, catching the sliver of cold blue light that came from inside the house. In this picture of the school's gifted-student team, Phúc is in the front row, her medal around her neck, her outstretched arms draping the shoulders of the two by her sides. *Cow-eyed Phúc.* I'd recognised her the moment I took the picture from the shelf under mum's altar in my house this afternoon. But I didn't remember where I stood. There was no time for scrutiny with the baby raising hell, so I just thrust everything into the outer pocket of my backpack. Mum's replacement slapped her child's buttocks: 'You tough crier, you.' I left by the back door, went through the small kitchen, pungent with pickled mustard greens, and walked the length of the garden border to mum's tomb. The quicklime was of good quality, the whiteness still fresh after months of rain. Only the gravestone had developed fine cracks. Thirteen in total, I counted, tracing my fingers along each of them, then cut across the garden border to leave my house. The baby's cries could no longer be heard. I considered myself fortunate that I hadn't run into my father. And that I had found the photo.

I was not in the photo. But Phúc was there alright, clear as day. She was not in my class, but the entire school knew who she was. Not for her big eyes and thick lashes, and not for her mathematical excellence. It was for her puberty. She was *stuck* around that time, the literal meaning of the euphemism used in these parts for that time of the month. The blood that people avoided, hated, tried their best to conceal, Phúc would be caught with it sitting on a tamarind branch, skipping rope, or walking to school, the crotch of her trousers stained with wet or dried blood. Her neighbours gossiped about how her mother would ask around for a bit of vinegar or yeast rice whenever she wanted to make sour soup. She did keep mother of vinegar and microworms at home, but they would die a mouldy death at the faintest whiff of a *stuck* Phúc approaching.

That snippet of memory prompted me to look at her crotch in the picture. Who knows, she might have been bleeding the very moment it was taken. I remembered how one day we were all walking home from school in the first rain of the year, bareheaded and exposed. Phúc walked in front, and from her darkened school skirt, her watered-down menstrual blood streamed down her bare shins. So beautiful that blood was, melted in the rain. Mum always said it was dirty, but I didn't find it that way at all.

But the *cow-eyed Phúc* in my memory was only her thirteen-year-old menstrual blood. Not a story for my newspaper. She hadn't come back after the incident. The private lead that my bosses had managed to tease, out of the thicket of rumours and the miasma of gossips that sounded more like myths, had revealed only a name and a hometown, Yên Xuyên. 'Fortunately, we have a proud native of Yên Xuyên right here.' The department head looked at me as she said this. A look which carried the weight of an assignment. But all Yên Xuyên had meant to me was my mum and two siblings. My mum was dead. My eldest brother had disappeared somewhere along the Chinese-Mongolian border. My second sister was toiling away in some Cambodian casino. My father's new son with his new wife was probably approaching his first birthday. Mum's tomb was still fresh. My brain was a blank, so I just lay idly on the porch, waiting for the bats to emerge from the mango grove. Their wings darker than darkness.

Ly called me at five a.m., saying, let's meet early today, she had a doctor's appointment for her shoulder pain later. For the last six months she hadn't been able to raise her arm over her head. 'Phúc said she'd give me a slice of that holy man's heart to cure me,' Ly said, and I pictured her pouting, probably not buying that such a cure could be found. She was my former classmate and Phúc's cousin. Perhaps a possible source for fleshing out the story.

'Can't believe your ma died,' was how she greeted me. I switched from my stool to a chair, knowing that she'd found her groove. 'Crushed under baskets of mangoes, holy mama, who would believe it.' She had indeed. I sunk deeper into the chair. 'Whenever I saw her on the way to the market I'd think to myself, geez, this woman is invincible. A full basket between her arms, three more hooked to her bike. She could even ride one-handed as if it was nothing. And then what? Crashed into the irrigation ditch in her grove and died, just like that. Who would believe it?'

I looked around. No bats to be seen now that the sun was out. The rays would scorch their wings. I turned my gaze to the road and counted the bikes. One, two, three. Lost the count. Started again from scratch. One, two, three. Was that Nhơn passing by? He hadn't remarried, even though it'd been seven years since my sister left. The last time I saw him, at mum's funeral, he'd told me, sad as a puppy: 'Can't forget her.' I found his keeping faith as despicable as my father's making haste to end the mourning period right after the final, seven-week rite, to make space for his new bride.

At my eighty-sixth vehicle, Ly finally ran out of things to comment on mum's death. Probably she'd remembered that she didn't have much time. She asked me what I wanted to know about Phúc. Anything and everything, I said. Tall order, Ly said. Phúc was away for most of her youth, pursuing her education goodness knows where, and they only met once a year for Tết, at her maternal grandmother's. Then out of the blue, a wedding invitation. 'I don't know if she still keeps them or if she's burned all her degrees and books.' After that, Ly sat deep in thought for a while. Phúc gave birth six months and a half after the wedding, to a healthy, chubby baby, only he never smiled. 'A baby that never smiles is not normal,' Phúc said, and she poured all her resources into finding a cure, eventually selling her house and moving into a rental. Her husband had disappeared soon after the wedding, presumably on a diplomatic mission in some desert country. One day, praying for peace at the Arcane Pagoda, she heard the rumour that the heart of this Lord in this isle could cure any ailment. An elderly woman gushed about how a mere piece of his fingernail, preserved in white spirits, had flicked away all her aches and pains. Phúc came home, called at all her girlfriends to borrow money, and the four million and seven hundred thousand đồng she got sent her and the baby on their way.

'The day she left, my sister-in-law came back.' Ly looked up at the sun, and then, perhaps out of distrust of that celestial timepiece, brought out her own watch to check the time, all without interrupting the rhythm of her narrative. 'Of course, she comes back all the time, she always tries to claim the bed my daughters sleep in. Says it's her bed. I protest, sweetie, you've been gone for so long, this bed's taken now, you can use the hammock instead. She says, sis, you know hammocks ain't good for a mother-to-be. When I was carrying my two girls, every time I took to a hammock she'd come back and vehemently shoo me out of it. But that day, I mean the day Phúc took my money and left, her heart-as-cure nonsense must have gotten into my head, so when my sister-in-law complained that her pregnancy had been stagnant for the last ten years without a bump to show for it, I blurted out: eat a human heart, your baby will grow in no time. I only said it out of frustration, but she hasn't showed up since. I can't help thinking she took me at my word and is off searching for a human heart somewhere. Now I don't know if I should still put sticky rice on her altar in the mornings or not.'

I tried hard to grasp Ly's story. In Yên Xuyên, my mind was sluggish somehow, as if doused with a mild sedative. Just enough to keep me hovering between falling asleep and staying awake. Ly was still droning on, tiny bubbles forming at the corners of her mouth. When I asked if her young sister-in-law was really dead, she gave a nonchalant smile: 'Dead as a doornail, she jumped into the river, my mother-in-law only knew she'd been pregnant when she said so the first time she came back. Asked who the father was, she said: the wind. She had a baby with the wind. Have I told you that her name is the same as yours? Only the middle name is different. Mỹ Phúc. I heard your half-brother is another Phúc, I don't know his middle name though. If your mum comes back, remember to ask her who pushed her into the ditch. Dying just like that, who would believe it.'

I made myself smaller in the faded plastic chair. Traffic began to swell around the roundabout, bikes running wheel to wheel, I couldn't count them anymore. But Ly's time had run out. She loudly sucked up the last millimetre of her drink and said that if Phúc was back in Yên Xuyên, she would surely let me know. Then, sighing, she said, 'My biggest dream right now is that I can reach around my back to unhook my bra.' It struck me that she was this close to trusting every remedy offered to her, if all doctors failed. Recuperating in peace at last, I realised that I couldn't manage one single talk with another potential source right now. Everyone in Yên Xuyên was either my acquaintance or my mum's; they all knew about her death, still warm in the depth of that stream as steep as a ravine. I called my bike taxi driver to come fetch me, feeling like I was reaching out to a rescuer.

When I got out of the café, the rays of the sun were scratching at the Chinese houses. Mum took me there once to get black sesame soup, a special treat. The handkerchief she'd used to wrap her money in had had mango sap stains.

The bike taxi driver who would take me to the coach station was already waiting on my uncle's porch. It was hard to guess their level of familiarity from the snatches of conversation, periodically blotted out by the whistles of koels from the mango grove.

'Looks like a long rainy season, this year.'

'If the sky would give us its water, all our pots and buckets wouldn't be enough,' the driver agreed. I'm always irked by those men who ingratiate themselves with all types of clients, who run their mouth off, who grow their hair long and matted behind their neck, whose body gives off the sour smell of stale sweat. And I hated him for taking me back to Yên Xuyên. But when he asked me, all solicitous, to save his number, and promised to take me to the station at a moment's notice, I'd sensed that this was one who could fish me up from the bottom of a river.

Thanks to him, I revived as our bike crossed the Running Water Bridge, which separated Yên Xuyên from the city. My mum sleeping in her fresh tomb, my uncle drinking down bitter tea and breathing out bitter words, his dripping wife disappearing in and out of the kitchen with ellipses in her speech, I'd left them all behind. The driver was still trying to strike up a conversation, even though my sporadic ums and hums, already muffled behind the anti-dust scarf, were further erased by the wind.

'Let me tell you, sis, my woman's as jealous as they get, the nights I come home with red marks on my shirt we're sure to have burnt rice for dinner. And you know, sis, working this trade, you can't only take on the men. What can I do when my lady clients put on lipstick. And back when I did carpentry work, my woman even suspected me of having a thing with the owner's son. We were friends, this lad and me, nothing more. As pure as pure can be, friends ever since our first cries. That Phúc, he was born on the same night I was, in the same nursery, delivered by the same hands, and when the owner's small wife sent a man there, he mistook me for the big wife's baby and dropped a mother centipede into my bed. As fat as a big toe, my ma said it was, though I think she was just exaggerating. The big wife would bring it up now and then, never forget your foe, she used to say. I don't know about foes, but Phúc always remembered how I'd suffered in his stead, he was always nice to me, never bossed me around. My da was just a lowly hired man, and Phúc's mum was the lady of the carpentry shop. But he took to me alright.'

'His name is Phúc?' I asked, unconsciously fingering the name in my mind. Away from Yên Xuyên, my brain was beginning to thaw, its gears picking up.

'Yes, sis, Trường Phúc, surname Lý. Now where was I, ah, my green-eyed monster of a wife, well, me and the lad did the things kids do, and she found them all suspicious: sleeping in the same bed, bathing naked together, giving piggyback rides to school when his leg was broken. "You were always finding excuses to rub up against each other," was how she saw it. Even when Phúc ran away from home, she thought she smelled something fishy. "Jilted boy fled the scene." What could I do, I'd already told her a dozen times and then some, he'd only waited for his leg to heal, and if he hadn't got away then it'd soon have been broken again.

'The owner's wife did everything she could to prevent her son from becoming what he wanted to be. Weeping, pleading, shouting, beating him, locking him up for days without food. She'd got pregnant with Phúc at forty-six, but kept the baby thinking to keep her man from straying further. She put her life on the line. You know, sis, giving birth at that age is three parts good luck and seven parts bad. Your kids ain't just your flesh and blood, they're your weapons, was what my da used to say. And now, each time my woman decides to punish me by taking the little ones to her parents', I think how wise my da was. Heck, did you see that kid on the bike? Kids these days, a bunch of daredevils. You never know what your own are up to when you've not got your eye on them. I swear!

Where was I, ah yes, the big wife's fortune changed in a heartbeat with Phúc's birth, not that the owner forgot his way to the small wife's place. He had a carpentry shop over there too, also named Trường Phúc, Trường Phúc no. 2. Same size, same level of expertise, same kinds of contracts shared out between them, only thing that couldn't be split was the tracwood bed, so it stayed in the master bedroom with the big wife. Carved with Chinese dragons, it was, and my da was the one chosen to help the carvers, royal carvers invited all the way from Huế, who told him on a tracwood bed you sleep deep and never have a bad dream.'

'And then? Did Phúc come back?' I asked, a slanting gust of wind distorting my voice. We were passing the Main Market now, and I was afraid I would miss the end of his story.

'Aye, that he did. But if only he hadn't. He could've gone and been a woman wherever he pleased, and I wouldn't've had to clean him out of the workshop shed. Even now my heart shatters just thinking about it. How can my woman imagine that I looked at Phúc lying there naked on the wood shavings the way a dog looks at a bitch. You'd have to have seen it to understand, sis, the shavings soaked through with sweat and blood, those sweaty carpenters walking out of the shed, Phúc lying there like a puppy torn to within an inch of his life.'

The driver fell silent. I couldn't see his face in the mirror. Was his story over? This kilometre was about to conclude, wasted.

'My name is also Phúc,' I said, hoping to pick up the thread. The driver resumed his story.

'I swear. Our people just love this name, both girl and boy can have it. So, every time I meet someone called Phúc, it reminds me of my old friend. No word of him after that day. I myself left the workshop. How could I continue working under that cold-blooded woman. Can you believe, his own mother locked him in that shed, she set her furious workers on him, and when I wiped the blood from his body, she was leaning against the doorframe, she said, "You want to be a woman? See how you like being a woman?"'

'What kind of a mother could do that?' I exclaimed, loud enough for two bikers in front to look back, expecting a lovers' quarrel.

'I swear! I took Phúc to the coach station that day too. He didn't say how much it hurt, and I didn't ask. Six years it took for them to carve him into a woman, you'd think it would be the most pain he'd ever endure. When I heard on the radio that someone from Yên Xuyên was looking for a cure for her baby, I suspected it was Phúc, even though my woman said, your friend doesn't have a baby bladder. Who knows, I thought. You should see Phúc as a woman, sis, every inch a work of art. The curve of his ear alone was enough for me to swear off my chisel, the most blessed craftsman couldn't have shaped such an exquisite thing. I swear, sis, I got so caught up in the story I nearly missed the station. Which coach are you taking? I'll take you straight to the gate.'

'Which one goes to Vạn Thủy?' I said. A bat's wing of thought glided across my mind. I wanted to ascertain which Phúc had arrived at that reach of the river. *Cow-eyed Phúc* was probably not the only one. The thought gave me butterflies in my stomach. I don't remember if I said goodbye to the driver properly or just thrust money at him as I climbed onto the bus, like throwing away an empty water bottle. The bus pulled out of the station, and from the back rows came the sound of a child crying. She was pestering her mother for some candies, and her mother was trying to dissuade her with stories about gruesome tooth-worms laying in wait inside her throat. Such a beautiful voice the mother had, I imagined it flowing out of a neck so long, so smooth, passing a slender tongue so pink, between rows of teeth so small and even.

I don't know if I'd begun sleepwalking by that point, when the beautiful voice was soothing the fussing child and I fired up my laptop to type the first part of a story for my newspaper. Now, from a distance made of cold, hard words, I could talk about Yên Xuyên merely as a place, a place with no connection to me. I'd taken a picture of the picture of Phúc in the gifted team and emailed it to the department head, who said they would fix the torn bit on the national flag that hung behind the students. Ever since our 'demythicising' series resulted in a six-month ban, we'd been cowed, self-censoring, like bunny rabbits bleeding to death out of wounds that never heal.

I hit Send and fell into a slumber, not waking even when the bus stopped for the long mid-journey break. The driver's assistant had to rouse me at the final stop and tell me that we'd arrived at Vạn Thủy. I yawned, put my laptop back into my backpack, made sure I had everything with me, then got down from the bus and walked to the gate. The assistant ran after me and pressed a rag doll into my hand, saying, sis, you forgot this. I wanted to say that it probably belonged to the child in the back rows, but he was already hurrying away. Yes, the sleepwalking must have begun at that point, when I didn't throw the doll away. I took it with me and flagged a bike taxi to a ferry stop with a boat to the Lone Isle.

'You wouldn't last long over there.' The old driver sounded concerned. I waved away his concern with a smile. In my sleepwalking, I hadn't pushed my heels fully into my shoes or wrapped the scarf around my face. Twenty-five kilometres from the city centre to the ferry stop, he said. The surroundings grew more desolate the farther we went. Empty outdoor shops, torn market tarps, stands with only their frames remaining. Faded cookie packages and plastic bags floating dazzled along dust-caked streets. 'Rundown' is too grand a word for this ferry dock, where the driver let me off and sped away, before I had time to ask him to come back and fetch me before nightfall. Then a ferry-boat—which I'd known was a ferry-boat when it was just a speck on the horizon—drew near, and the ferryman said, been waiting for you for so long.

No wind, and yet I am chilled. The closed sky seems to be holding its breath. I find myself in a peculiar situation. Standing here on the ferry dock, looking over to the isle in its death throes, wearing dusty shoes, nursing a doll belonging to goodness knows whom. I'm from Yên Xuyên, and my name is Phúc.

THE WOMAN WHO ENDED AN EMPIRE

By Phúc Dương

Yên Xuyên, with its population of nearly nine thousand, is a small town enclosed by fruit-laden mango groves, on the river Huỳnh Thủy that silted up two hundred years ago. It is not a place favoured by avid travellers, boasting neither tourist traps nor national heritage sites, and the coach service from the city of Thổ Tây that used to go here a few times a day has been cancelled for no apparent reason. The old town centre consists of three Chinese streets thick with the smell of herbs and agarwood, but later development has seen a few new neighbourhoods springing up to the south, and recently several covered markets have been built. All in all, another nondescript town.

This town would have never attracted nationwide attention without the collapse of the isle to the west of Vạn Thủy, a place that in recent years has been gaining notoriety as a hub of social ills, ruled by a kind of a cult figure. The woman who put an end to that perverted 'empire', according to our own sources, is from Yên Xuyên, and her name is Phúc. No physical description could be ascertained, but those who witnessed the moment the isle collapsed into the river described a woman in her thirties, bringing along a child.

The town's family registration ledger lists 117 individuals with Phúc as their first names, attesting to the popularity of the name in these parts. The town authorities themselves could not specify which Phúc might have been the woman at the centre of all the recent rumours. Adding to the confusion, more than ten also have the same family and middle names. The list, which stretched over five single-sided sheets, felt like a labyrinth confronting me. After ruling out certain people based on their gender, year of birth, and family situation, it was narrowed down to seventeen women in their thirties, with children, who are not currently present in Yên Xuyên. A few more filters, regarding the time those Phúcs left and the condition of their children, left four possibilities. One of those four women may have gone to the isle to the west of Vạn Thủy. I say 'may', because it is hard to be certain of anything when the main character is still out of my reach. She has disappeared after taking the heart of the one who called himself The Lord. A name and a hometown don't say much; she might have been living in Yên Xuyên, or she might have been born here only.

But everyone who attended the Yên Xuyên High School around the end of the last century assert that the one I am looking for must be their former schoolmate Nguyễn Hồng Phúc. *Cow-eyed Phúc*. The nickname evokes a daydreamer, one so absent-minded as to lose money out of her very hand. 'Well, what can I say, she was indeed known for writing in the air as she walked, all those formulas and calculations she was doing in her head,' said one of her friends, 'but she was so sharp and tight when it came to numbers and figures, not an airhead at all.' Phúc was good at maths, always the leader of gifted student teams in provincial and national contests. With a national award in her graduating year, she could have simply walked into almost any university of her choice. No news of her reached Yên Xuyên from when she was eighteen to twenty-eight, as she was away at Hà Đô, immersed in her study for a MD degree. 'She's becoming a professor,' her mother once boasted to her fellow vendors at the market, a fortnight before she handed them an invitation to Phúc's wedding. 'She didn't sound like someone who was sharing good news,' one of the market ladies recalled.

A surprise wedding is always ripe ground for rumours. Many believed that it was a baby-trap situation, given that the groom hardly smiled during the festivities and disappeared soon after. Or that the groom was a hired actor. That Phúc had attempted to take her own life when jilted by her professor. Speculations abounded, but none explained how a person widely considered to be 'highly educated' (meaning ample opportunities for jobs in renowned hospitals in big cities) chose to be contented with her life as a shop assistant in a department store in this rural town.

Asked about Phúc's time in Yên Xuyên after her confinement, a friend said, 'What can I say about her that's not also about me: groceries, meals, laundry.' How indeed to describe a normal person leading a normal life, the same life led by all married women with children in this town. Phúc surely didn't look like someone with a dream banished to the back burner, as she sat there behind the register at the store, in trousers stained with baby pee and blouses with traces of milk. Her mother looked after the child during working hours. In the pavement market near her home, Phúc had a reputation for driving a hard bargain, always asking for that tiny extra bit of vegetable or rice, and never too impatient to wait for the last notes of change. The only thing that betrayed her whizz-kid past was her astonishing skills at mental maths, 'no calculator could keep up with her'.

Her landlord confirmed that she was never late with rent, even after she had quit her job at the store and spent her days knocking on doors to find medicine for her child. People had tried to comfort her, telling her that not smiling is no disease, but to no avail. It got worse after her mother's sudden death from a heart attack, which took away the last reasonable voice by her side, and she began to pursue all kinds of miracle workers, charm healers, dancing mediums.

A refrain that I heard expressed by Phúc's friends, relatives and only brother alike, was that they can't comprehend how a medically trained professional could become so lost and bewitched by superstitions. A heart is but a mass of muscles and blood vessels, how can it be a miracle cure. The younger brother, whose view of the media is less than friendly, said that you journalists can keep trying to make whatever outrageous thing you want out of it, but his sister set out to take that heart simply because she believed it could make the baby smile. 'Apart from her devotion to her baby,' he said, 'the world can go to hell for all she cares.'

(To be continued)

CHAPTER FOUR

calling aloud

Báo and Phủ are no strangers to me, yes, they both grew up in this here Mud hamlet after all. They call it the neighbourhood of Nhật Quang now. Sun's Ray, yeah, that doesn't half grate on the ears. And that bridge over there, what's wrong with a name like Monsieur Scribe's Bridge, what on earth were they playing at to replace the old sign with a flashy Minh Hải? Shining Sea? Do you know they even tried to rechristen End Market a dozen years ago, but good luck getting any young or oldster to call it Farmers' Food and Produce Market, no thank you, End Market's plenty good enough for us lot, so all their effort went to spectacular waste.

Back to Mud hamlet. Forty years ago, it was this dark and dreary purgatory of a place, every night you would hear howls that might have been either spooked dogs baying at moonlit shadows or humans getting hacked and knifed, because the gangs would be out all night with their machetes fighting over control of the dock. You wouldn't survive here without fighting, the living fighting over food with the living, yes, but also over space with the dead, people would build their houses into burial grounds and cook on stone tombs, it happened all the time. The Mud kids played with tombs more than they did with each other. Little boys grew up to be gangsters, little girls to be gangster's molls, all roads led to the gangs. Weaklings became minions, strongmen bosses, like my old man who died in the self-same fake tomb which'd served as his hiding place when the going got tough. You'd never have known to look at it; my mum and I didn't even know there was such a thing; only a few of his close aides knew, one of whom later became my husband and replaced my pop as the dock's overlord, until the raids cleared out all the local tigers.

In those days the dust children flocked to the dock, as innumerable as stray dogs, and like stray dogs they came and went with no rhyme or reason, there in the morning, gone in the evening; the only ones left under our roof were Cô Long, Phủ and Báo, an unrivalled band of fingersmiths. You can count me as one of them or not, just the same, all I did was stay home and cook for the cubs, and put betadine on their wounds, nothing more.

Phủ was the prized apple of my husband's eye, the money machine of the trio, and also a trickster so skilled he could fool himself into believing his own tricks, he outshone even the geniuses in wuxia books; when he acted the student he was the most studious of them all, wearing his book-smart, innocent air even at home in the evening, where he would read well into the night. Even now the dock veterans still recall his dejected look when he picked up one by one the notebooks the baddies had knocked out of his hands, and held back his tears at the sight of his inkpot disappearing into the river; you'd be wrong to say he had a knack for acting; he didn't act, he embodied. When he played a dandy, all his hard-earned money went into fancy eateries and billiard halls; you'd find him in front of the Hòa Ký noodle bistro, one hand in his trouser pocket, the other putting a high-end cigar to his lips.

No wonder he believes he's immortal now, I said as much when I heard he was letting people cut off bits of his fingers to worship; and it was no surprise to me when Báo stayed behind on the isle, devoted to cultivating his friend's madness, he can't help but wait until little Cô Long comes back, she's the only one who can put an end to it. I keep imagining that woman, pale as a ghost, coming back in a rain that rocks heaven and earth, and then everything just disappearing. I'm over eighty now, I don't sleep much, I have all the time in the world for my whimsical mullings.

Báo came to visit me just the other day, enthusing: 'Cô Long is coming back soon.' He seemed so jittery, he didn't light the Hero I gave him, just sucked at the cold butt and breathed out imaginary smoke, he said he's been smoking imaginary cigarettes for so long he's got used to it, there's no cigarette or tea left on the isle, actually there's nothing left, those people have cleaned it out, even Phủ's shrivelled heart on a stake is waiting for someone to claim it, planted on the spot where his throne used to be, and now the waves are reaching that spot already, very soon the river will erase everything, cover the whole isle as though it had never been.

All were biding their time waiting for Cô Long, not that that was her real name, she never did tell us her name or where she came from, but Cô Long was the name I gave her, that girl as pale as Xiaolongnü from the wuxia books, pale not for lack of food or sun but as if it came from her very blood, the blood of someone who lives out their life inside those ancient tombs. I once gave her a copy of *The Return of the Condor Heroes* and told her to read the part where Yang Guo first meets Xiaolongnü and see if the girl in the book wasn't just like her. The girl made an earnest show of reading, I say so because she was illiterate, all the teachings in the world couldn't get into her head, but she knew the books in the shop like the fingers on her own hand, never mistaking the tome she'd hidden her booty in when pursued hot on the heels into the shop. Few people ever came to borrow those books, which weren't for reading, and from which I myself kept away as much as possible to avoid my husband seizing my hair and hitting me, my reading apparently a sign of disdain towards him. The same man who in my old man's time used to peep at me reading from a distance, entranced, later found faults with my literacy and education. Things had been in chaos ever since my pop's death. He was stabbed in the heart, at very close quarters according to those who knew about such things, when he'd pretty much dropped his guard, and on his pained face was also a trace of astonishment. His death left my mother and me reeling, we who hadn't nicked a fingernail working in our lives, at a total loss about the days to come. Three and a half taels of gold was all we could glean from around the house, everything left from our visible and hidden resources, and my mother could only think of two ways to keep us afloat, one being to purchase a lending bookshop for a small but stable income, and the other to marry me off to the new boss of the dock. 'If you become his wife, I can open a gambling den and pocket the fees,' she said. But since her talent consisted solely of dancing at the halls, her business plans followed one another to the ground.

Her lending bookshop languished in this motley hamlet of illiterates. And what her gambling den earned her she herself gambled away in a flash. She died a few years later, but I kept her books as a smokescreen; the cubs could just slip into the shop and then walk out clean as a whistle. If you knew the right switch to flip, amid all those identical bookshelves, one would open into an ancient Teochew tomb, connected to a maze of tomb after tomb into which they could vanish.

Little Cô Long didn't need to act innocent; innocence radiated from her whole being, even her pale skinny hand pulling a Miracle Hand Seeking Silver on the pocket of someone fresh off the ferry-boat was the hand of innocence; if conscience is ever made flesh it'd be that girl: pale as a ghost, with her long streaming hair that made her small face even smaller, and six toes on her right foot. You couldn't guess what she was thinking from her face, but my husband said dust children never think, and if they did, their thoughts would be about how to live through this hunger, and how to avoid being hit too much. I remember how he was fingering the hem of his shirt caked with dried blood as he spoke, presumably from thrashing a kid who'd made no money that day.

Báo was regularly on the receiving end of such thrashings, but all his bruises couldn't teach him to improve his own brutality, his kicks were still shy and his slaps clearly reserved, and their usual scene at the dock attracted the throngs it did only thanks to Phủ's heart-rending cries, so convincing that no one could resist drawing near, and Cô Long would begin her round when a crowd had formed, one toss of her hair and money would change pockets, all the while wearing a face as serene as the sky, even when the boys were caught red-handed she would continue to walk blithely through the crowd, nonchalantly tossing her hair.

I'd never once seen Cô Long smile, but Báo protested. 'She smiles lots, she smiles every time I give 'er a hairpin.' The buffalo-nosed kid was head over heels smitten with the girl, he poured all his meagre literacy into reading, specifically into reading *The Return of the Condor Heroes*, wherever Xiaolongnü makes an appearance, to compare the two Little Dragon Maidens, with a resounding verdict that the wuxia beauty could hold no candle to the living, breathing one.

During all those long years, the only time I saw Cô Long lose her cool was when Báo was arrested. The night before they sent the kid away to the juvenile delinquent facility, the girl clawed at the gate of the police station until her hands bled, and after that her face grew even paler and more impassive, never a hint of a smile or a tear even on the day she told me that she was pregnant with Phủ's baby, that they'd leave this life of crime, depart to the isle and plough a field out of the wilderness.

Boats from the dock ply the length and breadth of Vạn Thủy, and the Forgetful River keeps forking, sending out streams and channels to shape a multitude of inlets and headlands and isles, so many you soon lose count. I knew the Lone Isle by name but nothing more, all I could imagine was an isolated spot forsaken in the midst of vast waters and skies, and if not for the exodus of Phủ and his wife, I could have gone to my grave without ever setting eyes on it.

I visited the isle twice, the first time for the baby's first birthday, and to see how the young couple were doing over there; in that barrenness of an isle, they'd cleared a patch to grow some sweet potatoes; there were but a few families on the whole isle, it was so forlorn even a rooster's crow could startle you, and at night the laments of water fowl cutting deep at your guts. The second time was when Phủ had his men fetch me over to witness him on the throne before prostrating strangers, who worshipped him either because they genuinely believed in his holiness or because they wanted something from him, a scene I was sure would have pleased my deceased husband to no end, his favourite disciple playing god during a time when people no longer believe in anything yet are willing to believe in anything, but my husband had burned to a crisp in the bookshop fire after Phủ and

Cô Long left for the isle, rumour had it that it was arson and it was me, or else how could you explain the knife stuck shallow into the cracked corpse's chest. My fellow villagers would happily eat rice without meat, but their mouths itch if they aren't given enough gossip to chew. Back when I got married, they said that if my pop'd been alive, he'd never have let his golden daughter follow a gangster home, bosom disciple or not, the man would have had no choice but to stay away and swallow bitter saliva. It took my husband leaving in our nuptial night to go mark the woman Seven of the Ferry Dock with a knife to put a stop to the rumours.

The second time I visited, Báo was busy in the punishment house, with a woman from Phủ's chamber who'd been caught the night before with the cook; I didn't wonder how brutal Báo's beatings were or what form they took, such things were already plenty familiar. He only came out to see me off, still in his bloodied clothing; gazing over at the Great River he said, Cô Long must of departed from here, she probably didn't even look back when she untied the boat rope.

She was the reason Báo'd arrived at this place, I still remember the day he was released and made his way back to the dock, inquiring first as to Cô Long's whereabouts, second as to where she'd followed Phủ, and third whether the ferry-boat to Lone Isle was still operating at that hour, after which he made a beeline to the door, telling me he'd make a quick visit before catching the coach up to Red Soil to work carpentry with other newly-released inmates, but his plan didn't account for the sight of Cô Long at the door with a black-and-blue face, a face which showed no hint of a smile or tear at his appearance, a door which was slammed and after a while opened again into a house empty save for a bamboo-slat bed in the middle, where a drunken Phů was sprawled. Cô Long told Báo how Phů'd been like this ever since their lupus-stricken baby last convulsed in his arms, how he'd said, you don't even cry when your baby dies, so he'd been trying to draw out that cry hidden inside his wife's body, 'didn't you cry when he was caught?'

That'd been before they unearthed chests of gold buried at the feet of the sakae naa trees, which drew a flood of people to the small isle but drove away Cô Long, who'd seen Báo prostrating at Phů's feet and assumed it was for the gold, who hadn't stood near enough to hear him begging Phů to please take the gold and leave, just let her stay, and to this story, Báo added: 'she was carrying mine child at the time, I could of bowed before him til mine knees bled.'

That bow transformed the small isle. Cô Long disappeared, Phů assumed his exalted role, and Báo turned into someone that even I with my many winters was wary of. During those years at the dock when he'd received his daily thrashing with his meals, I would come to him at night to apply medicinal liquor and roll hard-boiled eggs on his bruises. If I was to choose one of them to adopt, it'd have been him, not the other two. But my husband had cut short that idea; humans are the most treacherous of all creatures, he said, it'd be like adopting a fox under your roof, and he looked at the knife he'd just thrown at the wall, the handle still shaking.

It was Báo who singlehandedly established the empire on the isle, he told me in whispers how from the start he banned the use of Phủ's name, it was just *The Lord* all the way; The Lord didn't give but *bestowed*, you didn't ask things from Him but *sought*; and he protected the precious godsend by a grim row of sentinels made up of fellow ex-cons who erected mansions and towers at his bidding. Following the scent of gold, all kinds of toughs and ruffians arrived at the isle, in response to which Báo orchestrated a succession of sensational assassinations whose outcome left the hitmen themselves awed, so awed they went around spreading the news that Phủ was a real deity made flesh, said they'd chopped him to pieces the previous night only to witness him back on his throne in the morning, nonchalantly accepting bows; little could they know that the substitute bodies had been dumped by Báo himself, down in the secret basement that he alone knew about.

'Phủ truly believes he's immortal,' laughs Báo. Every time he visits me on his motorboat, first he asks if Cô Long has visited, second he urges, master-mum, if you see anyone that looks like her please chase her down, third he enthuses, our child is definitely a girl. But that woman has vanished into thin air, so the trio's situation remains unsolved.

When I had my stroke the other year, Báo sent me a ton of ginseng and deer antler velvet to prop me up, saying, you can't die that easily, master-mum, you have to live and live long to witness Phủ's downfall, to tell the world that bowing doesn't necessarily mean fear, that there are bows that kill. 'Master-mum must know that better than anyone,' he laughed as he glanced towards my husband's face on the altar. Once he asked me if master smelled good, after the fire, 'meat is meat after all, must smell good when roasted.'

Old as I am, my mind a blind snail after the stroke, but I do vaguely sense that I too am a prisoner of Báo, who burdens me with the secrets of the isle, who turns me into the only, the final witness of this fantastic con, the sole purpose of which is to make louder the call Cô Long ơi, so that the girl can hear it from whichever edge of the earth she's ended up.

CHAPTER FIVE

water rising

Now water has engulfed Ash Hill, you look until your eyes fall out and all you can see is the same immense sheen surrounding you, to the left, right, and at your back. Water upon water upon sky, with no dividing line to be spotted in that continuum of slate grey.

I shift on my haunches to let my numbed dot-leg breathe, trying to keep my gaze focused towards where the hill had been until a moment ago. As long as I know Ash Hill lies that way, I can still locate the shrine of His Holiness, close on the right side of the hill, the Old Market to the left, and our village tucked up right behind the hill, its long tail trailing as far as the Cotton Trees curve. Beyond the end of the curve is where sister Tùy's house is, and her water-tap that's been flooding the village.

The first to discover the water running loose was the old ice-cream man. By then it had overflowed the washing basin and across the yard, pushing soap bubbles onto the road. Craning his withered neck over the dilapidated fence, the old man called out to those inside to warn them about the overflow but was met with silence. The one who'd opened and then abandoned the tap must have reached town by then, anxiously waiting for the train. The house had no gate, the door was ajar, and the only sound was that of water pouring upon more water. The old man walked away; he had no mind for strangers' business, cold winds from the North had been blowing and ice-creams had been staying unsold in his icebox, and his grandson had been whimpering for meat but there had been only boiled okra dipped in braised soy beans to be served at dinner.

'If only I'd gone inside and turned off dat tap, if only,' the old man kept chiding himself, later, when we were evacuating. As if he himself was an accomplice to the catastrophe. His belongings were tied to his bicycle in bundles, and perched atop his ice-cream box was his grandson, his face smeared with snot. Somebody consoled the old man, pointing out that if the tap could be turned off, we wouldn't have had to abandon our homes.

We were stragglers in the evacuation line. Old Keeps, who kept stopping and doubling up coughing. Me, who couldn't say how well I was doing with my semicolon pair of legs. And Tùy's mother, who was perfectly able-bodied but deliberately dragging her feet to avoid her neighbours' biting scorn, as the mother of a daughter who'd neglected to turn off the tap before running off with a man, the mother who hadn't stayed home to keep an eye on said daughter, and who had dismissed next door's kid when he tried to alert her in the middle of her four-colour card party: 'heaven can collapse for all I care; I have to break this losing streak.'

When she did get home, the water had wandered onto the neighbouring houses and washed away the herbal leaves that had been drying in the brick yard of the Hòa Đường Chinese apothecary.

'That good-for-nothing bitch, may heaven strike her dead,' the mother had howled when she waded inside, setting off waves that washed away the pot still encrusted with burnt rice, along with two mismatched slippers. Perhaps, embarking on her journey without much deliberation, Tùy had taken the wrong slipper. Perhaps she'd been lingering beside that basin over the rising bubbles, until a sharp call jerked her out of her wavering thoughts. Very soon, she would notice that she had on one brown and one red slipper, and perhaps she would remember the tap that she hadn't turned off. But it'd be too late; the train had taken her away long before those who remained came to realise that no one could fix that tap, but no one.

They called me over to try the following noon. 'The whole hamlet's given it a go, but no luck so far,' said the head of the hamlet. It seemed such a shot in the dark, no one really expected me to be able to do anything. They had tried plugging it with plastic bags, with rags, with pieces of styrofoam, but everything soon popped out and floated away. They had tried cementing it up, but the cement quickly turned to mush. They had even tried to block it by hand.

'It was like the water slipped around my bones to find a way out,' brother Five the Fearless said. His tattoos rippled over his market bouncer's muscles as he shivered. 'I'm still spooked thinking about it.'

Seeing him exhausted after his struggle with the water, I figured I wouldn't be able to do much, though I still pushed through the pointing, murmuring crowd and tried my hand at that tap, stubborn as a mule, its valve already broken and its body covered with dents and notches from what brutality humans had thrown at it. I was calf deep in freezing cold water. As if this water came straight from the underworld, itself connected to some ocean where icesheets floated.

'If only you hadn't mistreated the girl so much,

auntie,' someone said, and fingers began to point at the mother. They were all itching for a scapegoat. If only the mother had spared half a thought to give the girl a proper name, and not waited until the family registration officer needed something to enter in her birth certificate to snap out a single word 'tùy'—'whatever'. If only she'd given her daughter a proper education. If only she hadn't practically moved into the gambling house.

The villagers could judge the mother all they liked; the water wasn't about to let up. Daring, pig-headed, it was hellbent on travelling ever further. Impatient, the head of the hamlet went to see the vice district head. The two old classmates' reunion couldn't happen without an epic drinking party. When those two woke up, water had meandered to half of the hamlet. The vice district head, dress shoes hanging from his arm by the laces, went to Tùy's house to have a good long inspection, and then declared his conclusion, rather obvious:

'The water is coming from this tap.'

Someone suggested stopping the problem at the source, meaning the water facility. Someone else had the idea of digging a small canal to redirect the water to the Great River.

'Good idea, the river flows to the sea. One tap or a dozen, this will solve them all,' everyone said all smugly.

But there were no dozen taps to be fixed, only the one that Tùy had left running. And running. The canal that the men of the hamlet dug all the way to the Great River, nearly ten kilometres in length, helped coax the wayward water from going capering on the highway. People rubbed their hands together in happy relief. Apart from Tùy's mother, who had no way to overlook the goddamned tap in her own yard, the incident gradually faded from Old Market's collective memory. Until the day the Great River burst its banks.

Old Keeps asked me to help him move the worship items in His Holiness' shrine to a higher place. 'The water will rise higher yet,' he said, looking up at the sky. I suspected that His Holiness had paid him a visit to impart the secret knowledge. Mortals like me couldn't have divined how many showers were lying in wait beyond that sky, so clear of the faintest hint of cloud. The showers supplied more water to the already flooded fields surrounding the village. Field owners, after a hasty harvest, had to dry the grains on the roofs as all yards were under water.

But the exodus didn't begin in earnest until the visit of the province head and his entourage with their state-of-the-art equipment. Those devices can dive in on their own and handle the now deeply submerged tap. 'These babies can stop rivers, don't worry about your little tap,' the province head laughed as he crushed a smoking cigarette butt under the tip of his dress shoe, his immersion suit burning orange under the midday sun. Towards the afternoon, both suit and countenance had dulled somewhat, tinted with a certain embarrassment as the rescue ship made a U-turn to take the delegation back where they came from. They waved their hands and shook their heads. 'Can't be done.' To Old Market folks, those three words sounded like 'Time to run.'

The deluge, once opened, couldn't be closed.

At first, they wanted to move everyone to Ash Hill, but no way there was enough space. The hill could hold at best a dozen families, and that without their dogs and chickens and ornate wooden sofa sets. And climbing up there would be no small feat. That giant mount of coal ash, furtively dumped by some nameless factory dozens of years ago, had stayed looming in the middle of the village, worthless unto the end.

'It's said the vice district head has taken his whole family to Silt Land,' someone said.

The vice district head's choice must be a good one, was the consensus. And that was how it came to pass that Old Keeps had his permanent home at Silt Land after our long journey. If we had moved sooner, he wouldn't have had to walk through water all the way, succumbing to the cold before he could find a place to set down his brass mirror and set up a new shrine.

'The mirror stays, His Holiness stays.' I still remember what Old Keeps said when we were about to leave the shrine, how reverently he wrapped His Holiness in a piece of scarlet cloth, and then again in layers of plastic sheets. How he then tied His Holiness onto his body with his usual checkered scarf before putting on a shirt. If the old keeper stays, His Holiness stays, I remember thinking at the time. And I remember him saying on the way, think about it, kiddo, the water knows not poor from rich, facing its wrath everybody takes to their heels. He must have sensed how thrilled I was, with half my body submerged in the flood. With my semicolon legs hidden in the water, I was not so different from the next person. And now everybody was advancing on the road with the same awkwardness due to wading through fifty centimetres of water. Back then I thought, if the flood just remained at this level, no higher, I wouldn't mind if it lasted forever.

Back then, as it poured forth from the moss-covered tap that was fixed to a fence post with rubber hair bands, and meandered here and there down forking village paths, water still assumed the guise of a spirited child. Annoying, to be sure, but not threatening. People were swept up into its game, they put their rice barrels up on their bamboo-slat beds, until one day they noticed water lapping at the bottom of the barrels and shifted everything up onto the dinner table. It was such a yawn-inducing game of chase, you can probably imagine that water from a tap abetted by a few half-day rains couldn't have been fast enough to catch people off-guard. At times, the illusion was strong that the game had been broken off. 'Let's see who's the last one standing,' the villagers said as they waded through water to go to a fair in town.

But as we covered Old Keeps with dirt, fear suddenly struck. It was the stalking smell of death. Cholera came for the children, nearly ten of whom then died, devastating the people of the exodus. Gnawed by guilt for once having delighted at the prospect of a perpetual flood, I spent my days hanging around Old Keeps' fresh grave. I still remember his first words when he opened the shrine door to find me the orphan: 'How 'bout some white porridge with pickles, kiddo?' How he remarked that the semicolon holds a special place: 'It always introduces a very important thing.' And that the semicolon is the most neutral punctuation, it neither proves nor puts an end to anything, it never takes sides, it holds in equal regard both what precedes and what follows it. With a brain holding but a handful of words, thanks to his remarks, I felt less resentful of my footprints in the mud. I remember how he used to loudly snap his fingers and announce: 'We're eating meat today, kiddo,' and dressed up to the nines, he would go out to perform his rites in the worship chamber, where oracle-seekers awaited divine communication through his crescent-shaped brass mirror. Old Keeps was the only one who could see or hear anything in that dull, scratched surface. I had looked into that blind mirror a few times and seen nothing but a shadow wobbling, yet asserted that there were clearly a few sleepy vultures. Old Keeps said I was a bright child and the shrine would be mine to inherit. Ten years I had stayed there, but I never asked his name.

No one knew the name of the old shrine keeper. They only realised that now, sitting beside the corpse that was already growing cold.

'You've eaten so many shrine meals, what do you mean you don't know it?' somebody berated me as they rummaged in the dead man's belongings for something that could identify him. Not a single scrap of paper was found. The shamefaced gravestone just read Shrine Keeper, and the date of his death. His very age was a cipher.

His last words suddenly came to mind when they stood looking out at the watery curve, like a blister on the horizon. High as Silt Land was, it was no match for this flood.

'Do you remember Old Keeps's final words: the tap can only be stopped by the one who turned it on.' What the old man had spewed forth between two hacking coughs was repeated with the reverence befitting a divine message. That demonic tap had been gushing on, its water by then claiming hundreds of kilometres. They had assumed that it would abandon its game when it grew bored or tired. But this is water from the underworld from burst subterranean streams from dammed up rivers and those wouldn't stop, and Silt Land would surely fall come the next rainy season. They sensed that their woes had only just begun, and this flood was long from running its course.

'So we bring the girl home,' someone said. 'We can't run from this flood until our breaths give up.'

As luck would have it, we knew just where to find her. A phone call told us that Tùy had been seen wandering over in Vạn Thủy. Apparently she had been carrying a baby going in the direction of that isle. Probably her child. The child was not well; it was oozing water. 'Not a disease without a cure,' the mother said. The caller had asked if she remembered that she'd left the tap on, 'it's flooded the whole land'. But Tùy seemed to pay no attention, just adjusted the cloth covering the baby, who showed no signs of life, 'they say there's someone on the isle whose heart can cure anything.'

'You're the reason the Old Market folks are exiled from their land,' the caller had tried to implore her, all in vain. Tùy only said, 'My boy will be healed and roam the places, just you see.'

That precious call, from an Old Market woman who married far away from home, had made the search for Tùy as easy as pie, or so we assumed. All we needed to do was to phone those provincial officials to ask for their help, a simple matter of locating her.

'That girl is our only hope to thwart this water calamity,' the vice district head concluded his call in stern emphasis. But from a distance of nearly a hundred kilometres, the province officials couldn't see how in earnest and solemn he was, and slammed down the receiver in anger. Thanks to the flatness of the land, water had reached the provincial seat of power, and all the city's resources were tied up in evacuation efforts. No one believed that a random woman could stop the water calamity.

'Someone will have to go and find the girl.' After days and nights sighing at the ever-swelling water and the long silence from the province, we decided to take matters into our own hands.

And I was the chosen one. The only one with no business to tend to, and no family save for Old Keeps, who was already disintegrating six feet under. People of the exodus were all incredibly busy. In this strange land, we had a job just to put food in bellies. Every charity kitchen was already thronged with flood evacuees from Liquor Bridge, Neem, or Hanging Banyan, who had all convened here at Silt Land. Supplies were running low. Not to mention dry thunderstorms heralding the fast-approaching rainy season, meaning tents and camps would have to be reinforced.

'We will be forever indebted to you,' was their final blow as they pushed me onto the boat, facing the waterlogged plain ahead.

'I need something to tell the time,' I said on the eve of my departure, watching brother Five the Fearless breathing on his wristwatch and polishing it to a shine. Greed unbidden swelled inside me as I waited for a boat to be found. *Being seen* was a dizzying experience. Hitherto unheard words of encouragement and support were heaped upon me, 'here, take some more rice, you'll need strength on your way.' Friendly slaps on the shoulder and trusting looks emboldened me to make demands.

'This cock would be lovely company on my lonely way,' I clicked my tongue at the Divine Cock crowing triumphantly in the hamlet head's lap. My covetous gaze gently removed from his hand the undefeated gamecock, whose mighty legs each bore three rows of armour. The more precious the thing was to its owner, the greater my hunger to deprive them of it. One morning, passing a mother cooing to her baby, I got this close to plucking the nursing child from her breast. But the thought stopped me, what if, instead of drying up, the deprived mother's milk created another flood. The rogue tap Tùy had left on had taught me to be wary of all womenkind.

Thus my boat departed, laden with treasures commanded by my perversion. A crowd was drawn to see me off at Cotton Trees ferry-dock. I knew that their waving hands and tearful eyes weren't for me, but all the same my feverish mind envisaged a hundredfold crowd waiting on the dock the day I would return with Tùy by my side.

Intoxicated by that vision of me the hero, I failed to anticipate that the Divine Cock would be of no help in getting my bearings and the golden watch nothing but a dead weight when my boat ran aground on a rooftop. In the past, I would simply have followed the course of the Great River, but its banks were invisible now. I tried to keep the sun to my right so I'd know I was going North, but didn't plan for my only compass being shrouded with the coming of the night.

Thus my journey was stalled, but I knew when the night passed the sun would be up again in all its resplendence, greeting me from above the gilded waterfield. It would be my crutch to get to where Tùy was. And keep the faith the sun does, it always returns, even behind the thickest curtains of clouds it signals to us with its hazy glow. But the boat was faithless. One day I woke up to find it gone.

I had spent the previous night on top of Ash Hill. If it hadn't been for its tip poking just above the water, I wouldn't have realised that I was passing above the Old Market. With every roof now hidden, every village looks the same. But the sight of Ash Hill in the afternoon glare had awakened in me a childhood animosity and my old urge to take a dump on it.

'His leg is like this because of that wicked hill,' my mother used to say when concerned bystanders saw her kid dragging his dot-and-comma legs along the road. And so I took every opportunity I could to try and climb the hill, wishing to squeeze one out on top of it. But you may well imagine how scaling those sheer walls was beyond my misshapen legs. The mystery of Ash Hill wasn't only that it had appeared overnight, but also its height, which made people rack their brains wondering what it could be made of. I'd forgotten the old feud the way I'd come to accept that cursing the hill wouldn't straighten up my semicolon shins.

But that evening, passing the village and seeing the

hill on the brink of yielding to the flood, the old feelings stirred in me. This is a gift from His Holiness, I thought, and the brass mirror seemed to glow aflame under all its layers of wrapping. The Divine Cock, after days being confined in the small boat, was overjoyed at the prospect of clawing solid ground.

Later, clinging to a power pole and watching Ash Hill gradually vanish, I thought, I'd never won this fight. That night I had tied the boat rope to my own leg, because there was no tree on the bald hill. Before I drifted off to sleep, I even thought of the first thing I'd say when I met sister Tùy, which would have her follow me home without a second thought.

'If you can shut that tap, your baby will be cured.'

Perhaps she wouldn't believe me at first, so I would consult His Holiness to show her. Desperate people cling to whatever crazy nonsense is offered them, that's what Old Keeps had said when he passed to me his brass mirror, 'you'll earn your livelihood alright, kiddo.'

Plans always go without a hitch in our imagination. It hadn't even crossed my mind that I'd be hard-pressed to recognise Tùy even if I did happen to find her. You know how, to a kid without a home or a parent, who lives his life on His Holiness's charity, women are like fabled creatures living beyond the ocean. To a kid with semicolon legs, they might as well be living on the moon. I'd never felt like I'm worthy to even look straight at them.

The only thing I could be sure about Tùy was that she was neither one of the prettiest nor one of the homeliest. Or else I'd have remembered her from the few glimpses I'd had of her. She had a way of fading into the distant blur of girls, all with the same arching ponytails, the same brown sugar complexion from a native ancestor hundreds of years back, the same postures sitting behind market stands or sewing shops or disappearing in and out of inns. They are there and yet they are not. At times, certain portraits would crystallise out of the hazy dreamscape as one kills her husband another gets lost in Africa another contracts an incurable disease another nurtures a fatherless bun in her oven. Suddenly it came to my mind that Tùy smelled of bruised tangerines. Why tangerines and not the pickled mustard greens she sold at the market is a mystery. Her mother, the only person who might have clearer memories of her, had run off the moment our exodus stopped at Silt Land. She knew how hard life would be under the relentless judgement of her neighbours; whichever way you spin it, the flood had started in her yard.

'But there's still that watery baby,' was what the Old Market folks came up with after a long fruitless endeavour to jog my memory. 'Follow the trace of the baby and you'll find the mother.'

Millions of babies are carried on the streets every day, but there can't be many that ooze water. The problem had a simple solution. I would find Tùy for sure. The thought buoyed me on my way as I leisurely relished the magnificent exhibition of all those rooftops, normally forgotten and banished, a world where only cats roam. Now I could appreciate their beauty and individuality, those moss-greened shingles those patchwork iron sheets those leaf thatchings fortified by plastic. I could feast my eyes on them as the boat passed further into a world afloat. Floating prosthetic leg floating plastic table and stool many a floating cat floating altar photo floating pillow floating book and even a floating car. The Great Floating. A few Styrofoam boxes floated by, and I guided my boat next to them to look inside, who knows, perhaps there would be a babe for me to rescue and raise to be a true master, like in that movie they showed the rerun every summer.

But that was when I still had my boat. After finding it gone, I spent the whole day in a stupor, lying deep within the debris. Now I would make a pathetic return in a rescue motorboat, without Tùy, and without the brass mirror, my livelihood. With the mirror, people at least seek me out in moments of desperation. Without it, I would spend the rest of my life invisible.

'They're counting on me, they said,' and that thought lifted me up. I could stay put right here, to fix in my mind the location of that hellish tap. Then they wouldn't waste any time looking for it when Tùy comes back. She will come back, I believe, once she has plucked the heart of that dude she's looking for. Even if the rescuers see me too soon, they will have a hard time wrangling me out of this spot.

But no one went by. All around me was water, expansive, flat, still. So subdued and elegant, I couldn't find the heart to resent it. Once it had burbled happily, then it had hollered angrily as it barrelled down every hollow it could find, but now, having conquered all surfaces, it reposed with supreme calm, holding whatever mysteries in its depths.

'The same with humans, they grow taciturn as they grow up,' Old Keeps's words suddenly rang in my mind while I swam the dozens of metres to the power pole opposite. Ash Hill had fallen. But as long as I can keep my gaze fixed in same direction, I can still locate the Cotton Trees curve under that spot of water. And a short way beyond is Tùy's house, where the tap keeps pouring forth.

The damning thing is, I'm so sleepy now. The numbness in my good leg has subsided, as well as the chill in my bones and the persistent hunger that has been keeping me awake. Everything has given way to a profound drowsiness. No good news, this. Such a sleep cost me my boat. As usual, the catastrophe was preceded by a dream of growing wings. The process takes up the whole of the dream, which begins with a splitting between the second and third ribs and ends with lush thick feathers. It is a sorrowful dream. I have never been able to fly in this dream. And it was the same last night, the moment I flapped my wings, I was there wide awake and bare naked, of the cock of the boat of the hero bringing back the long-lost maiden.

I think I haven't mentioned that it was after such a dream that I woke up to find myself parentless, an orphan at the gate of the shrine. Or that Old Keeps also breathed his soundless last beside me when my dreamself had just started to furiously itch at the roots of my ribs, where the wings were beginning to stir.

CHAPTER SIX

cocoons

Around the middle of July, I heard that my big sister Thu had gone to Vạn Thủy to take the heart of some cult leader. The one who informed me claimed to be a reporter for *Tropical Bulletin*; he called from a landline asking for more information about the woman named Trà Thị Thu, 'after all, you are her family'. I told him that family comes in all kinds of flavours, Thu and I haven't seen each other for a long time, and I didn't know anything about her.

'Is she your sister or not, man?' the informant tried one last shot, texting from a different number. I read it as I got off work, wondering if it was meant to convey surprise, or provocation, or both, not registering how much I was disturbed by the question. Perhaps my body was just in that kind of exhaustion that leaves both the mind and the senses less agile than they should be. I reread the text in the takeaway diner while they were boxing my few purchases, and now the same words seemed covered in a fine layer of dust. He struck me as the type who always has dinner with his whole family, huddling around a small table, so small some of them have to wait for the second round while more vegetable is being boiled; a few siblings, married, live somewhere not too close yet not too far, who show up every weekend at the main house where the family altar is, chatting busily as they prepare dinner, after which the men settle at the table feasting and drinking while the women go out shopping, or sit around eating sour fruits with dipping salt, keeping half an eye on a gaggle of children. They know each other the way they know their own heart. The kind of people I had seen in an ad that enjoyed incessant reruns last Tết.

And those phony amicable faces, that showy coziness kept playing in my head on the way back to the house that had been mine six years ago. Now it belongs to my sister. In the twilight everything looked the same as it had been, the spikes upon the wrought iron gates, the blue-and-white striped awning, the areca tree in the yard, pretty much unchanged from the time I would walk in and out daily, but the sense of intruding into a stranger's space still held me back for a while on my idling Vespa. How I wished the lights would be on inside so that I could leave, convinced that she hadn't gone anywhere, that the call and the text were just a malicious prank. But the house was darker than darkness, a depression in the street where lights were now gradually winking on. I called Hào and asked if he had heard about anything happening to our sister, to which his intermittent answer was, somebody called but I didn't catch it all. The sound of keyboard clicking punctuated my brother's reply, suggesting that he was holding the phone between his ear and his shoulder. I couldn't think what to do next. Calling Tuyền was out of the question; at a distance of twenty hours by plane, in a place where even now the sun was rising, he is always wary of phone calls from the country he left aged ten.

No matter how long I lingered here, no one was ever going to come and accompany me into the darkness, so I turned off my bike's engine and reached in through the bars of the gates to pull the latch. Just as I remembered, the gates were never locked, and the key to the inner grillwork door was hidden in one of the battered shoes on the porch. As the key bit into the metal lock, I wondered when those two things last came together. I didn't expect to get the answer that very evening, down to the clothes my sister had on the last day before she left.

She had been wearing a windbreaker, a bit oversized, like a man's, carrying a bulging backpack and a big cardboard box which she had to stretch her arms around.

Before closing the gates, she set it down on the pavement so gingerly, as if there was something very fragile in there, and if a living, breathing creature, one of utmost sensitivity. The reporter had said that she was carrying a baby, but that couldn't be true. Who in their right mind puts a baby in a cardboard box? She lowered herself on her haunches, raised the box as slowly as she could, and without a look back at the darkened house, walked away at her legendary pace, which had often prompted the neighbourhood folks' quip that they would empty their pockets to buy lottery tickets the day Ms. Thu walks a teeny bit faster because it is guaranteed to be a jackpot day. And I, who had witnessed it time and again, kept being surprised at how serenely she walked under the pouring rain on her way home from school. Over that distance of a mere two hundred metres, she got unhurriedly drenched, covering her chest with her briefcase containing her lecture notes, always black in my memory.

'I didn't expect Ms. Thu to have family,' the night-shift attendant said as I cracked the egg and dropped its content into my steaming store-brand instant noodle cup. He had suspected me of nefarious intentions when I spent too long loitering in front of the house. 'But you opened the gates like you knew your way around it. How should I put it...' he seemed to be weighing his words, '... like you had it memorised.' He lost track of me once I entered the yard and moved out of range of the camera. After that, when the whole house lit up, he figured a burglar wouldn't be lighting even the oil lamp on the outdoor Heaven's altar.

I had turned on every single light in sight. I was consumed by the fear of stumbling over a decomposing body. But the opaque fluorescent light helped me see that there was no corpse in the house, though there were plenty of roaches. Roaches everywhere. Unfortunate roaches that burst under my shoes. And that smell that nearly knocked me out was a total smell of roaches, their excrement, their vomit, moist dirt rotting in cardboard boxes all over the house, of dust, of old furniture, and of dry flakes of skin now landing, now hovering under the slowly spinning fan. The ceiling fan had only two wings left, slightly wobbling as they span. Cabinets empty, fridge empty, no mouldy remains. Roaches also covered the floor of her bedroom, young larvae milky white, mature ones so dark it was hard to tell them from the loose dirt. On her bed, a pair of pillows big and small, and another of body pillows, neatly arranged. No other sign that spoke of the presence of a child. I threw open every single door, to protect myself from the surprise of any pouncing monster.

Plopping myself down on the wooden sofa by the bookshelves, as winded as if I had climbed up out of an abyss, as I looked at a dogeared copy of *The Silkworm*

Keeper's Handbook and gradually stopped panting, I realised that my stomach was empty. My takeaway mustard greens soup and salty roasted ribs were still hooked to my bike, but there was no rice in the house to go with them. Through the low window, I noticed the steamed-up or perhaps smoked-up glass wall of the convenience store across the street. I crossed the street in the simple hope of something to eat, never anticipating I would find my sister there, in the form of a few fleeting images, caught and captured.

There were four cameras recording different parts of the shop, the most wide-angled aiming at the door recording as far as the opposite pavement, gifting me a glimpse of my sister as she was leaving. The store attendant said, how fortunate, the CCTV memory only preserves recordings from the last thirty days, 'it's lucky you arrived not too late'. There was no hint of sarcasm in his voice.

'It'd rained since noon. Only let up by the late afternoon. See, there are puddles,' he informed me while adjusting the few hotdogs, so dried and wrinkly they must have been on the grill since morning.

'How can you remember it so well?'

'My grandma died that very evening.'

I couldn't think what to say next; if this had been a movie, I would have said sorry and he would have said never mind. No one has yet thought of a way to freshen this kind of situation, so even cinematic masterpieces have to recycle the clichés.

'Her three-week rite is this Sunday. I think. I didn't go back for the funeral either.' He looked at me with something like sympathy, even encouragement, as if telling me there was no need for the usual niceties.

It was a slow night at the store. There was a permeating smell of seaweed coming from the rice rolls at the fast-food counter. Hy, whose name I read on the tag on his chest, copied the footage of my sister to my phone. He said there might be more shots featuring Ms. Thu, inside or outside of the store, 'I'll look, but it would take at least until tomorrow night. Will you be back?'

I was back to see him the following night, when the flow of customers began to ebb. It was as simple as walking across a street pregnant with wind and misty air. I hadn't left my sister's house, and not only from being detained by the day-long rain. It was just that it was also so empty at home, I mean at the apartment Hữu bought in his name. He had gone home to his wife for the weekend, during which time, as agreed, we refrain from all contact.

Even during the day, my sister's place didn't look

any more alive. It was partly because of the rain, those soaked clouds hiding the sun. I recalled how once I had advised her to chop down the starfruit tree right by the window, so that there could be light inside. She said her roaches don't like the light. She had begun to keep Dubia roaches in two big boxes near the outside yard. 'These babies don't need much maintenance,' she said, lovingly nudging the boxes with her foot. What she did with them, who she sold them to, were questions I was just not curious enough to ask, as my mind had turned to mush at the sight of the shiny bean-green silky pyjamas wrapping her body. Cool, soft, smooth, flowing things always drive me out of my mind. Last night I had fished out that very outfit from the bottom of the drawer, and the stink of roaches didn't deter me from putting it on, slithering into her bed, and watching again and again the footage that Hy had snipped out for me.

We had done the same thing seven years ago, my sister and I, in front of the computer playing in a loop images of my father, captured on the CCTV system of an outpost beyond the Border Mountain, his last images before he disappeared. The camera he had around his neck was later found dangling from a low-hanging banyan tree. His shoes were left beside a small creek, two kilometres down the mountain path, full of some butterfly's cocoons. The disappearance was briefly reported on by a local newspaper before passing into oblivion. My father was a failed photographer, who lapsed into obscurity after his first award. In this era where digital manipulation can whip up seamless graphic feats, he still hunted for those moments of rarity. He would lie unmoving for hours on end, letting the mosquitos feast on his body while he waited for a flock of painted storks to cross the vermillion disc of the sun, or train his equipment for an entire day on a sal tree to capture the moment a flower splits from the stem. Those pictures, the fruits of his time-forsaking labour to freeze a drop of time, were then sold at a laughable price to magazines which splashed them next to articles singing the praise of our beautiful countryside, reminiscing about rivers replaced by urban spaces, wallowing in a sentimental, dated rusticism.

In the footage given us by the outpost, my father looks like a runt. The camera had been installed on the high central arch leading into the barrack. His face cannot be seen behind his wide-brimmed hat; his journalist's vest holds a water bottle in a side pocket; his camera with its 18-200mm lens rests against his left hip. Passing in front of the barrack gates, he stands hesitating for a good half minute, and keeps glancing down at his feet. The young soldier at the blockhouse nearby maintained that my father had stepped upon a cake of cow dung. The dung had dried around a deep footprint when the rescue team came across it. A roommate from the guesthouse where my father was staying had phoned Thu after making a police report, 'Mr. Bang hasn't been back for a few nights now, his money and papers are all here, I got a bad feeling.'

'Are you sure that's my father?' my sister had asked. The Border Mountain is such a distance away, nearly a thousand kilometres from home. When did he arrive there? We all thought he was leaving for Water Chestnut Fields.

I was there when my father announced his trip. 'Don't bother to leave out dinner for me for the next few days,' he had said. Those were his final words to us, and every time I think about them, I always reckon it's a decent enough farewell. When my mother heard the news on the phone, she laughed: 'Must've been taken away by the she-monkeys, that mountain's famous for its widow monkeys.' My mother has a way of making light of everything; even when she split with my father, to marry the man who later took her and Tuyền to the States, she summarised her nineteen years of marriage with a pithy 'Getting hitched early is best; plenty of time for a do-over.'

My father's disappearance did not have much effect on us. Even before that, he was seldom at home. My sister maintained that he was still alive somewhere, and steadfastly refused to set up an altar. Hào said he had never seen father alive without his camera. 'Accept it, big sis, dude's croaked.' Tuyền just let out an exasperated sigh on the phone. He didn't even remember what father looked like.

I took my brother's side in favour of an altar; that was after I had moved out to live with Hữu as husband and wife. With an altar at home, at least I could drop by once every few weeks to burn incense for my father and offer him the fruits he liked on a plate; I would see my sister's back as straight as a ruler at the desk as she marked her students' timed essays, or find her in the yard sweeping tiny blooms from the areca tree. This particular tree, of the variety often found in the gardens of country folks who still chew its nuts with betel leaves, boasting a slender trunk and a height that would twist the neck of anyone who tried to squint up the crown, had been planted by my father after one of his photography trips. Hào said the tree was a symbol of our sister. 'Don't you see how she's as erect as that tree, looks neither a woman or a man, never strike your lighter near her or you'll catch fire.' It's true that her high-bridged nose and large round eyes could not compensate for her stiff, cold face, her wiry mop of hair, her parched figure, and on top of that, the complete absence of a smile. My brother said no one would marry a woman too lazy even to curl her lips. Later, I would marvel at the way the two of us used to comment on our sister's appearance the same way the neighbourhood folks did, who said if Mr. Bang could marry off his ice queen of a daughter, they would give double their usual wedding gift money.

As far as I know, her students did not hold much affection for their literature teacher. They were put off by her strictness and not won over by her passion, which didn't ever shine on her unsmiling face or through her tone of voice. Her lessons must have been an exhausting affair, where teacher and students endured one another with boredom and hostility on both sides. Not that literature is a subject favoured by many kids: in this era of moving pictures and instant images, they get impatient when asked to do the imagining for themselves.

Her expression in the three sets of footage preserved by the convenience store CCTV matches the person I knew. Her tight-lipped profile makes her look as though she had lost her teeth. I showed Hy a photo of her at ten years old, hugging little Tuyên, a broad smile occupying her face. People often take the girl in the picture to be me. I had turned the house upside down before realising that my father had taken very few pictures of his own children, and none at all of the family together.

'Kids are always happy,' Hy said. His accent alone, hinting at a homeland to the north, told a story of adriftness, intimating that the young man had landed here after much travel, leaving behind a faraway land of dry wind and roasting sand. He had managed on his own in this city of strangers, working by day in some industry that he preferred not to talk about, and by night in this convenience store where he started last April. He had taken to watching the CCTV footage from the day just passed as a way to fight the endless nights and eye-watering yawns. He told me that he once saw his own little sister walk into the store with a man, but on the phone that night she had enthused about how she was at home watching over the family buffalo, who was about to give birth.

'You know, we really don't know much about our own family.' Hy spoke to the big monitor split into four small screens, the bottom right holding my image. Store attendants aren't allowed to chat with friends at the register, so I had to stay at the customers' table along the front glass wall. Nursing my second can of beer, nearly empty now, I watched the gates of my sister's house.

In another footage Hy had unearthed, timestamped two days before my sister left, she is wearing a sky-blue áo dài, probably on her way home from school, and lingers in the first-aid aisle before going to the register. Hy said the tip of her index finger was always wrapped with a band-aid, what does that tell us, apart from the fact that she was always bleeding? The day before that, an afternoon, wearing the same sky-blue dress, she buys a black hair band and at the register looks up straight at the camera for nearly a minute. But apparently she wasn't looking at the camera itself, but something beyond. In spite of myself, I walked to the register and mimicked her gaze. There was nothing there but three blood-red eyes staring back at me, suspiciously, or perhaps intimidatingly. My final image before I disappear from this earth will also be kept for thirty days by some electronic eye, before dissolving into the aether without a trace. And who will rewind my images?

I left the store at two a.m. Hy was still engrossed in the screens and didn't look up to say goodbye, but he would see my image pushing open the glass door and walking out into the street, a little unsteady from the beer. Inside the house, I searched for him through the low window, found the tip of his head above the revolving stand bristling with lollipops, and recognised a yearning in my body. Did my sister ever feel this way, drawn towards that young man who was separated from her by a single street?

I woke up her sleeping computer. On the browser, *Kung Fu Hustle* was paused at the point where the main character has just been killed and his weeping friends are wrapping his body in layers of fabric. Anyone who has seen this old-time movie would know that he is then resurrected with his power mightily amplified. I pulled up her search history and found, among others, 'insects with beautiful cocoons' and 'African lungfish', which reminded me of the white roll of fabric I had found earlier that day under her bed, and the book about keeping silkworms. For whom did she want to make those cocoons?

Meandering thoughts about my sister sent me off to sleep, until a tingling sensation came all over me. The light was still on and my bleary eyes registered a brown blanket on my body. The roaches. They had all but covered me, only my face was free. After a moment of freezing terror, I jerked up violently. The roaches were sent flying, and in the blink of an eye they all disappeared beneath the bed. Only the largest remained, latched onto my fingertip, swollen with my blood.

'I'm not her!' I threw the creature against the wall, where it burst. My own scream woke me up. I lay there in a pool of sweat, waiting for the dawn to break and for my dream to fade from my skin, picturing my sister walking back and forth around her house and talking, about the thunderstorm the previous night which had felled the flamboyant tree at school, or about her student who had dropped out to farm marijuana in the mountains. Was she talking in human language, or in roach?

The sun was rising now, and the roaches began to move

towards the boxes and whatever dark corners they could find. I grabbed a handful of them and turned them belly-up before locking the door. Those useless creatures just lay there, their legs swimming in the air, helpless. But still I ran. Another day here, and I feared I would no longer look at them as the weak, cowardly, stinking things they were. That I would miss, instead, the tingling pleasure of being covered by dream roaches.

Hy would see me when he started his shift tonight, the captured me who would close the gates, draw the latch, drop the key into the garbage bin nearby, then get on my bike and hightail out of there.

CHAPTER SEVEN

a cry from the sky

Those days would have been miserable enough for the four of us without the torment of the baby's crying. Hunger. Hungry we sat, hungry we lay, hungry we breathed. In between the hunger throes, an agonising regret, if only we hadn't run away from the camp.

'At least we'd be fed,' said a short-winded voice, I didn't know whose. The house was dark, and the only door led straight onto the main road, meaning that opening it would advertise the fact that a pack of escapees were hiding here. Even with our watermelon stripes stripped and sunk deep at the bottom of a canal, we couldn't just go swanning around in broad daylight, not to mention the frilly dress on Five Five One that he'd swiped from some drying pole. Bloody sod couldn't pass up a chance to reconfirm his status as a good-for-nothing.

And he was the very reason we had ended up here. The work group in charge of loading the acacia hybrid logs onto the truck was nearing the final layers; the ripened sun was about to fall down behind the cajuput forest; another day was nearing its glorious end, with the promise of the cleansing of mud under the cool water tap, dinner, the television hour in the common yard, and the oblivion of sleep when we leave this beaten-up corpse behind. But all was thrown into disarray as Five Five One abruptly took flight with not a hint of hesitation, each step sending up water like a shower of diamonds. And some sort of trance had come upon all the rest, who scattered like a startled nest of epileptic butterflies. Without a look back, we mad men ran raging on the reeds near the edge of the swamp forest, wading across canals of water as red as blood, crawling over patches of water spinach that pulled at our legs, until the guards' whistles could be heard no more. I couldn't remember how many forest miles how many canals how many reed swamps I crossed before collapsing on my abused legs, exhausted lungs heaving. There was a hint of blood in the smell of mud; those green blades had probably had a field day on my flesh. The foursome looked at one another, all the rest having either run another way or got nabbed. And I wished I could die then and there when Five Five One gasped out that he had only been chasing a fucking fisherman bird. A bird of such hallucinatory blue, he didn't know if it was real or not, he had to make sure for himself. 'But why youse lot all ran after me?' he asked. He wasn't immediately pounded to death for the sole reason that our drained arms couldn't do our boiling blood's bidding.

'I ran after you to tell you not to run.' It was Hiến who replied, his voice trembling with a hint of tear. He had realised—his sly fox's brain had instantly computed—that whatever the reason, the guards would never trust us to tell the truth should we return now. Even we could never trust this fellow with his dead-fish eyes. Every workday he managed to get himself the shadiest spots, the lightest carts of dirt and the smallest logs to carry. Altruistic acts are the farthest from his mind.

It was hard to trust him, because he was the one who roused us before dawn the next day. He said we first had to find something to replace our watermelon stripes, and then a safe hiding place, somewhere the camp warders would never think of. So we sneaked into this abandoned house on the road leading to town. Police sirens hunting for us blared from time to time, so frequently we lost count. The house held an ungodly amount of either tar or asphalt—in the pitch black all pitches look black—all dried and concrete-hard, in barrels half- or nearly empty; the house must have sheltered the work crew who laid the road through the forests. They had left the house so reeking of tar it sealed your lungs shut, but Hiến said that was a good thing, 'those mutts probably won't be able to sniff us out now.'

But tar is not nutrition. Hunger bleached our faces. The house didn't hold much in the way of food, apart from a few misshapen pans with the bottoms burned. A packet of instant noodles, its corner bitten off by rats, for a paper-thin lining of our stomachs; some bottles of already mouldy beer, their caps cracked open god knows how long ago. I found a tiny amount of honey in a condensed milk can, which had to be shared around. There was also a banana tree with one bunch hanging low at the back of the house next to the canal, where we had removed part of the wall when we slipped inside, but they were still so green the sap would glue our mouths so hard even yawning would be a challenge.

Food did exist a few steps away from us, but it might as well have been the other end of the world. The hot and heavy smell of burned garlic wafted over from the kitchen of the carpentry shop. We even heard them chattering about the inmates at large every time a police car sped by.

'We free now, is what's important,' Five Five One tried to console us after realising the full scale of the predicament he had landed us in. But his attempts only incensed us further. Great bloody freedom, beleaguered by darkness and hunger and the ever-mounting stink of tar. Hiến complained that his growling stomach was making it impossible to think straight. We had rushed headlong into this prison break without the vaguest notion of a plan. Should we venture out in search of food, we might manage to evade human eyes, but canine noses would home onto this smell in no time.

'I dun wanna go into the Basement,' Three Six Four moaned. Here was one so taciturn I used to suspect he was missing his tongue. His wordlessness closed him off like a boulder, even sweat couldn't find its way out of that glistening charcoal skin in the hottest working noon. His breaking into words must mean a great deal of inner turbulence.

No one ever wants to be put into that dreadful place. Jailbreakers who get caught would be punished with seven days and nights in the Basement. The person who emerges from it would sleep on his haunches for the rest of his life, and on moonlit nights would erupt into long, drooling howls. He would eat less and work twice as much as others, an idiotic smile would perpetually be lit on his lips, and his eyes would be red to the very irises.

I once went through a night in that place. I couldn't say what was in there, because when morning came my memory was a blank. My identity, my birthplace, my reason for being in the camp, everything was wiped clean; I didn't have the slightest hint as to what my name might be. Since then, I have merely been Two Eight Zero, as naked as the day I was pushed out. I was crushed, and chopping wood or hauling sand for the new football field under the infernal sun was made worse by not knowing for what sins I was paying, for what transgressions I should atone.

Hiến was the only one of us four who hadn't endured an overnight stay in the Basement. He was too cunning for that. I suspected that his memory remaining intact was the reason he kept his wits about him. Memory is what makes a man a man. At the very least, he knew that this stretch of forest was surrounded by rivers on all sides, and that getting to a river would improve our odds of making a clean escape. We could cling to the sides of flowers-selling boats, and breathe through straws underwater to get past checkpoints. Or we could hide under all the floating mats of water hyacinths.

'I saw that in movies as a kid,' Hiến said. He might not have meant to boast, but nonetheless it hurt. The rest of us might very well have watched hundreds of movies and learned dozens of vanishing tricks, before everything was erased and we were turned into stale trunks of flesh. And Hiến was our brain now. He said we had to stay put and wait, then when the hunt eased up we could cover ourselves with tar and go out to find food, and a way to the great river.

Such a joke of a plan. But even that went down the drain when the baby's cries threw open the tin door. A woman appeared, outlined with light, and the squirming bundle in her arms was shrieking as harshly as the guards' whistles. We had been all captured by that baby.

I remember that she left as soon as she saw us, stunned, dive away from the sudden light, but soon returned with a thick stick in her left hand, before Five Five One had time to close the door.

'Elephants or wolves?' she said. What a puzzling question. Ever since my memory wipe, every outdoor shift I would pick a spot near an old prisoner who was a teller of dazzling stories, and I grabbed at those miscellaneous anecdotes to fill the void that was my mind. He had a veritable treasure trove of words, which I absorbed like a sponge. And I never missed a TV hour in the common room, hoping to chance upon something which would illuminate the darkened chamber of my head. All of which gave me sufficient confidence to say that I'm neither a wolf nor an elephant.

'Mice. We're just mice,' Hiến piped up from behind a tar barrel. I didn't even notice him slipping back there.

'Why not say we elephants to scare her off?' Five Five One whispered.

'And then this loony missus will go blabbing to the whole market that there are four elephants hiding in this house?' Hiến said through clenched teeth. That moment, I envied his sophisticated mind. Mine only came up with the simple thought that I was not an elephant, because elephants never forget anything in their life. One look, and they remember unto death. That's what the TV said.

'Mice eat my baby,' she asked without releasing the tip of hair in her mouth or the stick ready in her hand.

'Nuh-uh. Mice only eat rice.'

You must think this is all a load of crap. Four muscular inmates cowering before a woman, a woman not only bonkers but with a baby in her arms. Mother and baby together weigh less than half a man. We could snuff them as easily as swatting flies. But that would be if we hadn't run dozens of kilometres through the forests, on empty bellies going into their second day. The animal in us was lying in a pitiful, hungry heap, and at that very moment Missus Loony stepped forward to sprinkle some rice before Hiến. In a flash, our lifeline revealed itself.

'Mice also like instant noodles,' the craftiest mouse said, with a hint of embarrassment.

Missus Loony had no instant noodles with her, so she tossed us a loaf of bread torn into pieces. She must have thought mice couldn't cope with bigger chunks. But crumbs were no problem if they could stop my stomach growling. Or perhaps the growl persisted, but it was muffled by the cries of Missus Loony's junior. At first I thought it was just throwing a crying fit. But it kept whimpering even while it was nursing, and I began to suspect that this baby never stops.

Not until the second day did I realise what torture we were in for. The baby cried and cried with barely a second's let-up. Each new breath-holding attack further ground us down and shrivel our guts up. You know how a baby cries himself breathless, and in the silence between the cries you think surely this time he's shut up for real, or else he's perished. But those moments of hellfire kept coming back, reduced me to a handful of ash. Only Missus Looney wasn't affected, or perhaps she was, but she had no other recourse apart from chewing her hair, singing nonsensical words, or growling at the noises outside the door. Like mice who know their place, the four of us made ourselves small in a corner behind the barrels while listening with every cell in our body for someone to barge in through the door at any moment.

But there were not that many callers. Over at the wood shop all seemed to know Missus Loony. Some would poke their head in and sigh, such crying would surely lead to dehydration and death. An old woman selling fried rice balls asked, concerned but impatiently, if the mother thought the child had stomach flu. The girl who brought Missus Loony food twice a day always stopped outside. Through the crack on the wall, I could see the faint terror on her face. She must have felt the full assault of the cries.

'Don't go home ah, no one can bear that crying,' the girl said as she pushed the hot box inside with her foot. Her arrival would send Missus Loony into a fit of rage, one hand brandishing her stick and the other squeezing the baby to her chest, and she would growl, you eat my baby. The baby would let loose an ear-splitting wail in support of its mum, and the screeching blast would send the girl out of there in a heartbeat.

Wouldn't throw it to the garbage heap, would ya. Ma's head's still pounding. Ya just wasting time, a baby that cries like that's not gonna last long. Piecing together the girl's disjointed comments, we figured that this abandoned hole was a last resort after the crying had brought someone's house down. Missus Loony wouldn't compromise with her folks, she wanted to keep her child. Her family had had enough. Suddenly I felt so much for that girl. I knew too well what she had been through.

'Can't... sleep...', Hiến sounded desperate. I didn't know

if his remaining memory made him more vulnerable. Perhaps he'd heard or lived through many such fits in the life he'd left behind, and now who knows maybe they were all coming back to tear at him. Or if the baby's cries had dished out equal suffering to every one of us. Three Six Four was visibly disintegrating, the closed-up boulder having been cooked into lime. He said the kid must be strangled if we wanted to survive till the end of this month.

I myself couldn't think of a less cruel way out. The baby's eyes were closed tight, it must have been asleep, but the crying simply wouldn't stop. It just grew faint, a whimper like a coal flickering deep in ashes, apparently dozing but liable to burst back into flame at any moment. The TV said that people can only put up with loud music for a maximum of forty-eight hours, give or take, but this is crying a slow slicing a gradual drilling a tightening of the noose. The chubby kid looked the picture of health, its voice full and echoing, its lungs probably very strong and its throat a spacious chamber. Waiting for natural death to come to this hellish emitter of cries was asking too much of us.

This baby must be around a month old, Hiến guessed. He had a child of his own, who was just taking his first tottering steps the day the father came to the camp. Last he'd heard, the kid and his mother had moved to Stork Fields to raise free-range ducks.

'My child smells of rice off the pot. Rarely cries,' he said. Children is a perplexing topic to me. Whatever experience I might have had with them was erased down in the Basement. The cooks had kids, and kept a draconian eye on them in case they wandered near us pariahs. And the television didn't deem it worthy to show educational films about kids and how they grow up. Once I believed I must have at least a dozen, waiting for their father back home. But now, listening to this bundled creature's unholy din, I thought it's for the best I don't have any. I wished I had had at least one endearing baby-related memory, but this mad woman's child was all I knew. Squishy as a worm, sucking until swollen then vomiting it all back up, shitting stinky shit, peeing in an arc, and crying as if having bottled it up for seventeen cycles of lives.

Missus Loony did know that there was something wrong with her child. She gathered all sorts of nameless herbs, crushed them and applied the paste to the baby's belly. Sometimes she held the child upside down as if to pour out all the crying inside. She even licked its ever-streaming eyes. But still it cried on, perhaps to revenge the dozens of past lives it had failed to do so. And its mother went back to chewing her hair. Apart from her hair chewing, and sometimes picking at torn threads from the mat which lay upon the pallet floor, she was the same as any woman in town. Tidy and neat.

And reeking of milk. That smell was so strong it competed with the smell of tar, at times even eclipsing it. Hiến said that after a woman gives birth, they have to crush alcohol yeast in water, apply the paste to those arrogant mounds, and burn a bouquet of incense to dry and smoke them so that the milk inside will ripen.

'The milk won't smell good otherwise,' he was deep in another trip down memory lane, 'my child smells like sweet potatoes off the coals.'

At the time, we who had gone through the Basement didn't realise that Hiến was talking too much. We were mice alright, but mice shouldn't be too squeaky. He talked about his house, resting half on solid ground and half on poles planted in a riverbank replete with mangrove apple trees and fireflies. His child sits in a floating plastic basin which he would drag along in his trips setting up nets for climbing perch. His child has the pearliest of laughter. His child smells of cooked starch, of rice of potatoes of golden young cobs of maize. His child never cries.

The night Hiến disappeared, the baby raised hell with its crying. Towards dawn, we realised that our brain was gone. We didn't know if he had slipped out through the front door or where the back wall had been knocked down. Or where he had gone, if he was caught or had reached the river. Five Five One said, wherever Hiến was now, at least his ears were no longer being assaulted by baby crying. His voice was full of abandonment, as if to say getting caught is a risk worth running, and I predicted that he would soon leave too.

'Gotta strangle that kid to survive,' Three Six Four lay on his back looking at the ceiling, regurgitating, ruminating his previous words. It was the fifth night since our escape, and he and I were the only ones left.

At times, we had made so bold as to venture near the bamboo-slat bed where mother and child sat. But we quickly scurried away when she hurled some pieces of bread back to the barrels, signalling loud and clear that we were not to approach them. As stately as the true lady of the place, on the very first day she had gone straight to a wall and drew aside a wooden board to reveal an unexpected bathroom. She even knew there was a blanket inside a box under the kitchen counter. Sometimes, looking at her sighing while spreading her legs on the bed, I wondered if the baby's father hadn't been one of the construction crew. If the bastard even knew what a dreadful creature he had created.

There was never any opportunity for us to touch the baby. Whenever she went out to find bread for her two mice, she always took her child with her. She never slept; I think perhaps mad people don't need to. Because the lack of sleep didn't defeat her. She seemed lively and lordly as ever, looking upon us as a human looks down at an inferior species. Indifference, toleration, condescension, distance. The kind of gaze that ignited in us both impotent rage and suicidal humiliation.

Without Hiến to guide us, I figured we must devise a way out of this cell with its thick walls made of smothering cries.

'Your baby needs medicine so that it can stop crying.'

'White rain whiter than white moon.'

'They say that the heart of the living Holiness can cure all diseases.'

'Sun so sweet the dragonfly's sister sobs.'

Missus Loony didn't even appear to have heard me. Her nonsensical replies amused me enough to soothe my slow perishing. As I continued to weave a whispered tale about the healing heart of a man over at Vạn Thủy, lording over an isle filled with gold, I had no idea that my made-up story was the truth, and that the man himself had once survived my attempt to assassinate him.

Way later, arranging Southern medicinal herbs to dry in a mountain hermitage, eavesdropping on some visitors gossiping about a woman carrying a baby who had travelled a thousand kilometres to pluck the heart of the Lord in that isle for a cure, I didn't for a moment doubt the identity of the protagonist. It could be no one else. A mother just like all mothers, neat and tidy and reeking of milk, with a baby as soft as all babies. The only things that distinguished them were the mother's hair chewing and the baby's crying. Her hair, once so long and thick, might have grown sparse by now, because she would pluck out a strand every time the baby fell into one of its breathless spells.

She is the only one from that time I've heard anything about, ever since I stopped being a mouse and left that house, that claustrophobic hole that reeked of baby crying.

CHAPTER EIGHT

the shadow bride

'Bet you sisters won't see the end of that pile of logs anytime soon.'

I was looking over to where Xây and his wife were sawing logs, separated from us by a road on which sunlight had raised a wall to the heavens. Feeling I'd become a specimen, same as all the other women sitting there. Down to the bitter sigh hidden within the words, the anger tinged with sarcasm.

'If she'd only hold the other end of the saw, they would of got it done ages ago,' someone added fuel to my fire. As usual, the tongues of the Station Market women wagged sharpest when it came to the topic of Xây's woman, and I could feel welcomed into the fold.

We loved to lay into the road inspector's wife at noon when we sat around with our trays of cigarettes and mints, waiting for the train. The women would chatter even as they were half dozing off, their ears attuned to the sounds from the other bank of the Dry River, where the train would begin to slow down. It was the only train in a day that called at our Way Station. Between our yawns, we would gaze towards the road inspectors' collective housing, where the couple would be visible now and then in their tableau vivant of happiness. They were practically joined at the heels, together they stood, they sat, they plastered over the cracks on the front wall, they strung up their drying poles, they mended tears in the floor rag. They were the main course served up to those tongues that, idle at noon, sought to taste strangers' business. Looking at the couple whose hands kept finding new things to be busy at, the women fumed:

'Whatever way you look at it, that chap's always alone.'

'Can't expect much from a shadow, now can you.'

I'd known from my first days here that the gossipers would find my own appearance at Way Station a new delicacy to sink their teeth into, so I made sure to join the flock every noon and stay until the day's end. I only needed to hold firm, and I'd become one of them. As long as I was an accomplice to all the venom flowing through the noon market, I'd be safe however long I was stranded in this alien land.

Viễn had taken me to Way Station, and with a 'wait here a few days' he was off on the train. I still wasn't sure if Viễn was his real name or not. There was nothing in the house that betrayed his former occupancy. I clicked the lock shut then opened it again a few times, trying to use the rusty keys he'd given me to assert my rights to this room. The money he'd left me had evaporated within a fortnight, but one noon the train let out a boy with a face as sharp as a needle who came to find me with a new wad of notes. When asked about Viễn, the sour-faced boy snapped: 'you know he's away, so why waste your spit.' He managed to disappear behind the train door snapping shut right at that moment. I followed the departing train with my eyes, thinking, who knows, Viễn could be on that very train, but why there was no sign of the man, as if he'd been fully digested by it.

Back to the room on the edge of the collective housing, I peered into every nook and cranny, to make sure no surprise skeleton would jump at me from a closet. But the smell that I suspected to be bones was actually dust. The back door was blocked with a broom, which I didn't touch, just dusted a space large enough for me to lie down, hoping this would mean I'd soon move out.

'Other end of your row, that chap, he took a shadow for wife,' one of the women had said, her voice dripping pure contempt, the very first day I moved in.

For lack of anything better to do, I mentally trotted after the sisters back to the wedding that took place four years ago. Xây was stiff in his black suit, his manners somewhat strained, but his eyes couldn't contain the joy that covered his face with a cloud of jubilant mist. At the height of the party, a few maverick cows strolled by to eat the flowers on the decorative arch. A silly quarrel ended up inconclusive, over whether ghosts bite their fingernails.

I could see with my own eyes the sky that night, so black it bordered on invisibility. They had a night reception, two strings of lights across the yard, the bride now slanting long at the end of the yard, now bending all sweetly over the old wives at their separate vegan table. As if she didn't want to overlook a single guest. The groom's mother had a tad too much to drink, humming words that stuck like lumps in her throat. Out of despair, she'd thrown in the towel, surrendered to the god of alcohol, and slumped in a snoring heap by the chain-link fence.

They said that his mother quit eating the day he told her, in all seriousness, that he was going to marry his own shadow.

'Is there no other girl in this land?'

'I care for her.'

'You can marry blind Lê from the next village, at least she looks human.'

'Our wedding is fixed for the twenty-ninth.'

The Way Station women had nothing good to say about Xây's wife. 'Can't even smile on her own,' they said. She was too distant, she was there and yet she was not, she did everything with a lightness they found unbearable. She was worlds apart from the local womenfolk, she cleaved to her man, never a step away. At first her attachment drew admiration and praise, but gradually that turned into jeering: 'she'd choke on her phlegm and die a second away from a male, eh?'

'What did she ever do to them?' Xây once said, tears in his voice. He felt it was so unfair, the way his wife was treated. She did nothing, it was true; all she did was being happy. The kind of happiness that drives other people nuts. No woman loves to see another happier than them. They spat words of venom at her face. She showed no reaction; she expressed herself only through her silence. Silence so solid it built an armour encasing her, immune to all adversity. In fact, she did talk, but only her railman husband could hear her. Often people wondered what she teased him about to make him laugh so. Or smile his kind, amused smile. Their own sphere, their very private communication shut the door to the world outside. As if the very air they were breathing was different from the rest.

Shut out of that sphere, the mother would complain about her daughter-in-law to anyone who'd listen. That the lights were always on whenever she was home, that she never answered when talked to, never was so kind as scratch the old woman's back. That she was a clingy leech, who wouldn't let go of her man even when spat upon. One day when the wintry winds came from the North, the drunk mother slept in the station, caught a cold and died. During the funeral, someone related how, back in the day when the train still stopped for fifteen minutes, the old woman (who was a not-old woman then) would entrust her tray of cigarettes to a station sister whenever she snatched a guy into the shed. Xây was a gift left behind from some man's hasty visit, cut short by the drawn-out whistle of the departing train.

Viễn didn't feature in the women's village anecdotes. I decided I'd had enough waiting and bought a ticket, but then the needle-faced boy turned up with another wad of money, neither thick or thin but as stained as ever, and sourly informed me that Viễn wished me to wait until he came back for me. 'I'm late for a long while. Must be it,' my words were drowned out by the train's desolate lament. The boy let out a sigh, his face even more needle-like, 'Another mouth to feed'. That night in my dream, I saw a needle baby pierce its way out of my belly, its cries arrows shooting in all directions, making holes in all the walls around me.

For lack of distractions to while away the day, I attached myself to the station market, injecting myself full of venomous contempt for strangers' business, until the last woman had put her tray on her head and gone home. Over the road, Xây and his wife had closed their door, taken up their satchel and left to inspect the track, taking away my last source of entertainment. I was alone, disoriented.

I decided not to go back to that dusty room and walked the length of Way Station, this town with its many complexes, playing a guessing game using the drying poles. Bent after a day baking in the sun, the bamboo poles exposed the minutiae of each family's life. Men's shirts stained with rubber sap, women's sagging blouses, children's small items crowding their own poles, corresponding to the cries and quarrels coming from inside. Those women that'd been my world just now were flitting about inside those huts, roofed with iron sheets and walled with wooden boards cut from rubber trees that have given their lives' worth of sap. No one beckoned me to come on in. We'd been so tight, yet only moments later they saw me as an outsider. Each was trapped inside their own busy world, cooking dinner, preparing snacks for their husbands' drinking party or cleaning their vomited aftermath, or spanking their children.

Realising my evening idleness might incite hostile stares, I headed to the edge of town. Beyond the welcome arch, on which a wing had broken off, a small road led to the highway, but the forbidding barriers between the two allowed for no conspiratorial intercourse. With the highway refusing to open up to it, the road was a thin stalk dry of sap, with no hope of grafting to the branch. There I lost my bearings, I didn't know which way was home, I mean the house with the tap running into the washing basin I'd forgot to turn off when I ran away with Viễn. Only one thing could be sure now, it was too late to go back, that tap must have flooded the village.

I opened the back door. A few forlorn train cars, wallpapered over by a thick weave of morning glories, corralled a discreet yard. Where the railroad inspector couple had created a world of their own.

'They grow some vegetables, and put out a board bed to catch the night breeze,' I described the scene to the Station Market women, 'and at twilight they go lie there on top of one another, tight as clams.'

'Do they really?!'

'Indeed they do, with nothing on them, out in the open air.'

That mundane routine of theirs, I embellished a bit to spice it up. I was in possession of the only back door that looked onto the private world of our neighbour couple. And the miracle had happened, the outsider that was me had become the most sought after in the market. But then dusk came, the train departed in haste, the market dissolved and the trays travelled home in the women's arms, with hardly a cigarette sold. And I was on my own again.

One day, figuring if I kept trekking along the railway, with luck I'd catch some unexpected train rushing through, I walked intently between two hedges of poisonous oleander, entered the vast expanse of rubber trees that swallowed all Way Station's men each morning, and came to the dry bridge over the Waybread River, now a stream of dry stones, to Three Pieces Mound. As I was massaging my exhausted legs, the railman couple came up to me.

'If only she'd stay home and fix that sod's dinner,' I thought at the sight of the flickering wife supporting her husband's hand as he put yet another rock on the mound. A few rocks a day, the mountain's not far away, he said. Deep under the mound was a girl who had lain down across the tracks, meticulously preparing to set sail, resting her slender neck on the metal rail, making sure nothing would go awry.

'Her head was light as feather,' Xây recalled. It had also been the first day he went forth with his satchel of tools. The incident had occurred half a kilometre from his site.

'Her eyes still twitching like crazy, could of asked her name, but we panicked and it went clean out of our heads.'

I looked at his wife, disarticulated on a sleeper. She seemed to be smiling, or maybe not; she was mouthing what her husband was saying, word for word, as if she'd learned the story by heart.

She had been there, too, the day of the accident. They said that the fifteen-year-old Xây had been besotted by her magical way in which she transformed with the landscape, and the sun and the lights around her; the way she could create doubles of herself or shapeshift in the blink of an eye. He began to talk to himself in murmurs, and sometimes cupped his hand to shield some invisible companion from the sun, or jumped over a puddle and cried out in high spirits, I won. If held back for a chat, the youth would look anywhere but at his fellow human being.

He was never alone. Much later they got to know why, during his three-month probation as a railway inspector, walking forth and back for a total of twenty-two humdrum kilometres a day, in the beating sun and the pouring rain, he'd never once complained about the monotony of his work. And why the girl who enlisted the train's help to cut herself up on the very first day of his job hadn't fazed him at all.

'A human being, cut into three pieces, when put together, looks just like a train,' Xây said as he upended his water bottle into his mouth. And his wife naturally opened her beak in anticipation. How much water could quench her thirst, I wondered, pitch black as she was.

A train passed by us, scowling. An Unfaithful Train, as the Station Market women called those that didn't pull in at Way Station. The couple grabbed at me and pulled me back. The arm waving the signal flag was half shielding me from rushing onto the tracks, half hailing the humongous centipede. I watched the train send up a dust storm beyond Dry Bridge, thinking perhaps Viễn was on it, or perhaps not. Then it disappeared, leaving a fresh trace right before my eyes. A streak of mushy faeces dragged and dripped across several sleepers. I retched my guts out.

In the following days I kept retching, for no discernible reason. Of course, I discerned it alright, only I pretended not to know it. But the sisters at Station Market had no qualms about calling it by its name. 'Your morning sickness is bad, so it is, prepare to be miserable soon.' They were right. Water entered me and went out as saliva, air entered me and went out as dry heaves, and each somersault of my stomach left me flatter, more ground down. As if my stomach was hung above my head to drain. But still I dragged my haggard body across the station, blended in among the women, found some target for my hatred. A strong enough dose of passion to fight off the disintegration deep within myself.

My inexhaustible fountain of saliva had attracted a stray dog. He kept trotting beside me, scooping up everything he could. In between the heaves, I craved for rotten leaves, the kind used for thatching drenched with the smell of ant eggs, of rain, of lizard pee. I didn't expect that Xây and his wife would also be mesmerised by my sickness. It seems all Way Station women get pregnant and give birth as easily as they breathe; an epic morning sickness such as mine had never been seen.

They would hover at my door, entranced, watching me nibbling at the few rotten leaves newly foraged as if beholding an extraordinary marvel of creation. Every time I threw up, they would exclaim in admiration: 'Again, she did it again!' I felt like a monkey jumping through a fiery hoop, and they were the audience gaily applauding my seared hair, but I was too drained to be angry. They did what they did, and I kept puking and munching my rotten leaves, feeling the sweetness seeping into my marrow.

'Weird food, you eat such weird things,' he said, or she did, borrowing her husband's moving lips.

'Get a sickness or two, then you'll know weird.' Annoyed, I flicked my foot against the dog's flank.

I'd be reminded of what I'd said later, when the couple came to entrust me with their house keys, saying they didn't know when they'd come back.

'They say up on Orphan Mountain there's an old master of Southern herbs,' he laughed as he looked at her slanting long on the ground, 'she fancies a baby.'

It would be a long time, maybe forever, before I set eyes on the railman couple again; that knowledge was as evident as the fact that Viễn would never come back, it clouded my mind and choked any kind words I could've thought of: 'Tell the medicine man to tone it down a bit, a litter of ten would tire you out for sure.' But venom didn't require any thinking, it was ever present on my lips: 'Shadows beget shadows. You'll never be a human unless you eat a human heart.'

Was it because of those words of mine, that she went to the isle of Vạn Thủy?

CHAPTER NINE

fairy ascending

Twenty-six days before the conclusion of the first Year of the Flies, Cẩm left me, taking the baby with her. The day before that, I'd counted the number of days remaining as I ripped off another sheet from the calendar and said, with those strange flies congregating out there, the coming year was still a nebulous unknown. Things have been falling apart ever since their frenzy was loosed upon the world, and a calendar for the new year seemed the remotest thing now. Cẩm didn't reply, just glanced out of the window. How could I fail to notice how much more frequently she'd been looking out of the window those days. There was nothing out there, only a world of flies and fly shit. The golden trumpet trees, which'd had a few branches left when she'd arrived (she'd remarked on what a life of travail they lead, labouring to bloom all seasons), were nibbled down to their roots. Even the tangles of phone cords had had their plastic jackets munched clean, their copper hearts exposed, by those ravenous vermin.

Remorse gnawed at me for going through that whole day without realising her resolution to go. She ate more, nearly a third of *Light in August*, approximately two hundred word-filled pages. She didn't set aside the pretty words as usual. And her nipples were cold. When I drifted off beside little Mushroom, Cầm disappeared into the storage rooms. She went looking for the toy mask and those sacks which, together with the garbage bin still lying upside-down by the back door, eventually helped with her flight. Mortal men keep making the same mistake, not willing to just burn the frigging fairy wings. You burn them to ashes and then your wife has no way to fly back to her sky.

I'd completely let down my guard, for we were living in such leisure in this forsaken library. No toiling for our daily bread, no locking ourselves up within orders and dogmas, no keeping an anxious eye on the elements. It was turmoil out there, with the flies hankering for blood, the food soon running out, the mosquito nets, the Paracetamol worth its weight in gold. But we were separated from them by not only this wall but a thousand light years, in this paradise of the first golden age. As long as air still seeped in through the narrow slits around the windows, and clean water still ran from the taps, we would still be living in comfort. This library, with its masses of volumes holding countless words, would sustain us for over a decade more.

We eat words. Please don't react like those vulgar folks I used to know, who'd look at me as though I was mad, or who fixed on me suspicious eyes, trying to guess at some hidden meaning beneath my statement. Eating words means just that, eating words. As simple an act as your eating food. To chew them with your teeth and savour them with your taste buds and digest them with your stomach and absorb their nutrition with your intestinal linings. There are probably plenty of other eaters of words out there; we just don't hear about them.

I myself had assumed that I was a freak apart till the day Cẩm washed up at my shore. By then, the strange flies' occupation of the universe had gone on for over half a year, and sometimes I got this human-longing. In such moods, I'd go and stand in the reading room, by the glass window dotted with fly shit, and watch the street below for an occasional passing car, a glimpsed human profile. A left or a right, depending on which way the car was going. The rich, immune to all kinds of circumstances, still traverse the city during the day, unfazed by the aggressive flies. Sometimes a car making a U-turn would drive into the library yard, and I'd get to see a full face. It's stressful to manoeuvre such unwieldy vehicles, and a middle-aged man's dour face was the last one I saw before Cẩm emerged from the upside-down garbage bin right by the window and looked up at me. Nursing in her arms a blue weak sound of crying, she was drained after a full night's journey with that bin on her head. It was only at night that the wicked flies' onslaught slackened.

Carless, Cẩm floated up to me in her garbage bin. It hadn't been easy; at times the winged enemies would spot her and she would drop the bin to the ground, laying low, waiting for a chink in their siege. Her baby was wrapped in layers of cloths, his cries now barely audible from behind his Hanuman mask. His cries eroded my resistance, and I found my eyes drawn to the door. That door had been opened only once, in the early days of the plague, for an addict couple who then came close to butchering me in their withdrawal throes. Back then, humans were still reeling at the sudden subversion of their dominance, but now everybody had learned how to exist in the flies' world. Cẩm was such a fast learner. Cutting a small window into her bin, wrapping thick canvas sacks around her legs, she'd managed to evade most of the bloodsucking flies on her way.

Later, Cẩm told me she hadn't had a plan when she set out, she was just going for going's sake, 'beats hanging around until death finds ya.' She said she glimpsed hope for the first time when she spotted me brushing my teeth through the glass.

'Nothing to eat in here,' I made a broad gesture of shooing her away, trying to fight back the baby's weakening cries.

'You must live on air, huh?'

'I eat words.'

'So do I.'

She said it with such casualness, I could detect no deception or surprise in her voice or in those eyes blinking wide. This woman admitted to eating words so naturally as if there was zero thought process behind it. And my wrestling the rusted latch off the door was out of pure curiosity: is it true there exists a fellow word-eater. At that moment, I didn't conceive of her as a woman, of warm loins, petite nipples, firm buttocks.

The building didn't feel any less immense with the new resident. Cẩm had assumed charge the moment she walked in, as if she owned the place. She never asked 'what should we have for dinner' the way my wife did every single day of our life together. I remember how I would offer her my trademark reply, 'anything's fine', and my wife, enraged, would scold me for being too lazy to even spare a thought about food. There was only so much enthusiasm I could fake for human cooking. I played along to pass the day, but by midnight, hunger would catch up with me. I would sneak out, take down a volume, and treat myself to a lavish banquet of words. No way to tell the books apart in the dark, so I just made silent guesses from the taste. Once, my wife caught me in a dark corner, chewing on half a page from *White Deer Plain*.

'I can't live with someone who eats paper,' she said as she plucked clothing off the pole to stuff into her suitcases.

'People eat ants and worms all the time, what's so bad about words,' I tried desperately to salvage the situation, though I'd known it was the end the moment she ran to her room and vomited her guts out.

At seventeen, when I first discovered I could eat printed things for food, I did wonder if it was the paper pulp my body needed. Or the mineral oil in the printing ink. But the blank sheets I tried were all too bland and tasteless, and the ink too gross to be palatable. I'd even tried paper and ink mixed together before coming to the conviction that words on paper are what satiate my appetite. But such nuances were lost on my wife, who found them all to be savagery.

'If one of us has to go, let it be me,' I said. The split was swift, as I didn't have much to pack. The crisp snap of the lock—the brand-new lock that my wife kept all the keys for—sent me on my way.

Cẩm laughed as I recounted the crumbling of my marriage: 'Should we avoid the word "ex-wife" now; you'll break your teeth on it.' On her part, she gave away nothing about herself or the one who'd fathered little Mushroom. She hid her identity and her past behind her protruding forehead, so big her face seemed to be broken right across her eyes. Her face was always closed even when her whole body opened up to me. But that was no cause for worry; days and months stretched ahead, plenty of time for me to travel her depths, a world unblemished by the buzzing of those strange flies.

The day our company folded, I'd picked up my tool bag and gone straight to this building under a gloomy fly-infested sky. We'd once been sent here to fix a busted water pipe. A rather loose door opened to where the pump was, behind the building. My hammer and crowbar made short work of the door, and I took over the building without breaking a sweat. The library was empty, just as I'd expected; they had abandoned all the books in their hurry to save their skins. One of the first places to be orphaned when troubles come. Who needs books in a time like this. Inside the office, I read the salary sheet, trying to recall the name of the unsmiling librarian I used to see. Perhaps she'd discovered that words were missing from the books I'd returned, or it was my baldness, or never smiling was a special mark of all librarians. Now, studying their meagre pay, I realised to my relief that it probably had nothing to do with me.

There were sixteen rooms in total, spread over three floors. It was dizzying to think I had the run of the whole place. I sat in the director's leather chair and spun like a kid until the room became a merry-go-round. I stamped all the documents and books within my reach with the scarlet stamp. I made squiggly signatures, none of which resembled any of the others. I threw open every door in my way. After a thorough search, I estimated that this store of words could sustain me for the next twenty years. Outside, the loudspeakers kept hounding citizens to shelter in place and keep their doors shut, their intermittent urgings talking about a world I no longer seemed a part of. I watched the news on the office television, feeling like I was tapping into communications from Mars. Then the cables were cut, and the incessant hail on the screen dropped a thick curtain between me and the apocalypse outside. On the last bulletin I was able to see, heads of states played the blame game as to the flies' origins; a professor informed us that it would be 'an opportunity for the human race' when the flies, pressed for food, began to turn on one another; the national police agency announced the presence of microchips in some dissected flies; and journalists documented the mass exodus towards the Heavenly Mountains, which showed no sign of letting up despite scientists' warning that there was no grounds for the assertion that the strange flies couldn't live at high altitude. In a split-second frame, I saw a fellow from my plumbing crew, definitely him, clutching the leak detector on his shoulder and tilting his face upwards for some fresh air amid the jostling crowd. It was shot from a high angle, and the images got scratched badly by the flies' flutters. I wondered what my colleague had thought when he brought along his equipment, if he really hoped to continue to ply his plumbing trade up on the Heavenly Mountains. During our farewell drinking party, he'd grabbed a fly and chewed it alive, saying, those are flies and we are men. He hadn't accepted defeat, even after he'd lost his job and taken miserable refuge at home all day to the sound of his kids crying and his wife scraping burnt rice from the pot. I wondered if he had now, as I was finishing the final pages from *Decameron*.

I was an indiscriminating eater back then. Ever since Cẩm's arrival, it had been a meandering feast. She is a connoisseur, and her meals are slow and deliberate, whereas I just take down a random book and chomp my way through it page by page. She'd give Mushroom to me to hold and then stroll about the bookshelves, all of them except the political aisle. She'd pick a few words here, a few there. If the love poetry felt a little mushy on our tongues, the lines carved from an essay would bring back balance. To top it up, there were always a few words she delicately cut out of pages printed only on one side. Rare, original, pure of taste. You know how the pages of a book are often printed on both sides; the words on the reverse side would be inescapably bound to those on the front. You think you're dining on a *young sunbeam* that smells of lemon balm leaves holding the last trace of the first dew of page 23, but tagging along on page 24 opposite may well be the word *shit*. Not a much-utilised word, perhaps for aesthetic reasons, but still a possibility.

Some words would be so beautiful Cẩm didn't have the heart to eat them, instead she'd painstakingly cut them out with a paperknife and put them away in their own drawer. Things like *languid moonlight softly spilling over the field still pulsing with lingering patches of the day* or *apples waning in the dark* seemed to smooth over her broken face under her protruding forehead. And I would be stiff with desire.

'The hand that wrote this *serenitude* must be a most exquisite hand,' she said, her face a portrait of innocence and purity of heart, like a girl of thirteen years who believes all the princes of the world are handsome twenty-somethings on the whitest of steeds.

I remembered one of my old man's drinking buddies, a poet from the provinces, dried and yellowed. Curious to see if his words were as yellow as the blood that seeped out of his mouth in the last days before he succumbed to a liver tumour, I'd searched for his books during my first days in the library. But his name couldn't be found on a single book. I felt sorry for the deceased poet; if only he'd spent a bit less time in rowdy company and a tad more on writing, on capturing every fleeting thought, to leave at least a handful of words behind.

Cẩm laughed again when I told her about the poet. 'Words come in all kinds and some are best left unwritten.' Once she pulled out a book and suggested we eat all the words that were superfluous. The ones that, taken out, wouldn't make much difference to the story. The book ended up with less than a hundred words left, and Cẩm commented on how we'd stuffed ourselves with empty calories. But with *The Burgomaster of Furnes* we couldn't eat a single word; the author must have been agonising over every full stop and comma.

The world out there could keep hurting, people could keep refusing to accept their own downfall at the hand of a lowly life form, fights could keep breaking out over rice and cough drops, but Cẩm and I kept feasting and loving between the tall shelves in the reading room. The gaze of Mushroom, who was learning how to crawl, didn't bother us. During those carefree days of ours, the only discord was the sound of fingernails scratching bleeding skin.

A few die-hard scabies pimples were popping up on Mushroom's body. 'If only I'd covered my baby well, those hateful flies wouldn't've bitten him so bad,' Cẩm kept chiding herself. I told her not to sweat over mere scabies, trust me, all kids go through a string of such ailments. Green snots, swollen worm-housing bellies, feverish lymph nodes in their crotches. Nosebleeds, full-body rashes, the odd dislocated wrist or cracked bone. 'No kid ever dies from such minor stuff,' I tried to comfort her, 'or scabies.'

But she wouldn't be comforted. She was often distracted, her mind circling around the child's pimples even as her body was mooring into mine. 'They look like volcano craters,' she said, fingering the high ridges around the deep ravines. We sharpened paper clips and hunted out the mites burrowing deep inside the blisters, but it wasn't enough. Night after night, apart from the sounds of restless scratching, there seemed to be an undertone of the mites tunnelling into the baby's flesh. Heaven knows what venom those flies had marked the baby with; these weren't our run-of-the-mill itch mites.

I recalled how the sun helps some, so at night I slipped outside to scrape off the fly shit darkening the windowpanes and put both baby and his clothes up to catch the slanting rays of the sun. Problem was, the flies were still there between the sun and us, ever ready to smother the rays.

'Our baby won't be at peace without medicine,' whispered Cẩm, the lower half of her face darkened in the shadow of her forehead. Mothers are always fussing, I thought, without realising that the flight was beginning to weave its tendrils inside her.

One day, I blew up when Cẩm, still mooring into me, reached out to rub the pimples on Mushroom. 'It's not the kid alone you love, but his father's part in him,' I said and went upstairs to spend the following three nights in the newspaper archives. Dining on those words, I understood why she'd once advised me to 'only touch them as your last resort.' On the fourth day, she called an armistice, carrying the baby upstairs and smiling at me from the doorway: 'I've laid out some very fine words downstairs.' That day, when we moored into each other for the fourth time, she said she would give me a child.

'Our child will also eat words,' I said as I stroked her leprous nipples. Mushroom hadn't been able to; when we tried to feed him torn-out bits he'd spit them out, or chew when we forced him to but choke afterwards. Without other food, he sucked his mother dry. Cẩm could eat reams of words without producing enough milk for a child in his growth spurt. 'He doesn't eat words because he's not my child.' I tried to keep the thought from surfacing on my face. You know what thoughts are like, sometimes they get wicked or dark; I was only human after all.

Until then, I'd always assumed it would be easy to love a kid that wasn't your own. All you need to do is remind yourself that this is a part of the one you love. I have to baby this baby, was the resolution I kept in mind. And I did, I babied him like a valued guest. But sometimes a minor grudge would let loose the thought that without the boy our paradise would be whole. Especially when her nipples grew all leprous when he sucked too hard. Her nipples were the part of her body I cherished most, tapering as small as the tips of chopsticks but never drooping. They were perky, proud. I was only allowed to dine on them after Mushroom had drained all her milk, but the taste of liquorice still lingered in my throat.

With her gone, I ate and ate and devoured all those beautiful words she hadn't had the heart to bite in two, but couldn't find again that liquorice taste from her small nipples. There was no alcohol to drown my sorrows, so I upended the garbage bin, trying to off myself on the words she'd discarded. I wolfed down all the *bereft*, *soledad*, *weep*, hoping for death to come and release me. But death didn't visit that easily, only a face-swelling allergy that lasted for a few days at most.

She'll come back when she's found a cure for Mushroom's scabies. That's my belief. But I can't hide out in this library much longer. They've cleared up the flies, or else those monsters are biding their time in their secret lairs, until their hour came round again. Heavens knows what wicked schemes they are dreaming up. On my TV screen, the grainy hail has ceased, replaced by the scene of Monsieur Ta Da at his golf course, signalling a universal revival. Before the librarians return, I've cut out all the heart-shatteringly beautiful words to put aside in a special box for Cẩm. I imagine how her sharp angles will mellow when she caresses the *afternoon reached down to the water as if to kiss it, drumming taps of the rain*. She will come back, that's my belief. Even after a note with her handwriting fell out from between the pages of *The Museum of Innocence* and slashed me in half with twenty words, 'Is it so, that because of those scabies bites, ever since we washed up, you have never kissed our baby?', I still believe that she will come back for me. Or maybe not.

That day when the radio broadcast that a woman carrying her child was seeking a human heart as a cure, I knew at once that it must be Cẩm. Now the problem facing me is, whether I should apply as a security guard at the library to stay until she comes back, or pack up to go find her in that land of a thousand isles.

CHAPTER TEN

no one comes wake up

'Twas just on a whim that Mi popped up at that isled region, believe me. Don't expect her to talk much about it, that is if you're lucky enough to find her at all. ' 'Cuz'—I bet a hundred per cent that's what she'd say. Same way she'd talked about the old denim jacket she was never seen without (even before we'd met, and perhaps also later when we were no longer attached at the hip), which was a sight to behold: candle wax describing geographical shapes on its shoulder, a long tear from the second button down, and the fabric worn to threads in places. First time I picked her up at the mansion at no. 2 Mỵ Nương Road, I'd taken her for the daughter of the gardener or a kitchen hand, but my mild condescension was soon turned to shame when people bowed low before her at Shake 'n Shout. You must know that place, still the poshest in town. More than half of the wine kept in the basement was hers, heavy platinum or leather-bound bottles. Just like you can't judge a book by its cover, you'd never guess her tattered jacket held a black credit card. Once, when Mi was squeezing the rain out of it and then hanging it to dry in front of the air con, I asked her why it had to be that jacket. ''Cuz.' That one-word answer was her explanation for each and every action. Sure, you wouldn't find it satisfactory, but if you tried to press further as for what goes after ' 'cuz', she'd smirk and say, man you really don't wanna head into that Freudian labyrinth.

I met her on the website cumocoi.net. Those children of the night, the orphan owls of the title, went there for companions to storm the streets, hit some spice, gamble, get pissed, or get laid. One night, Mi posted on the forum in search for a fellow jumper from Star Bridge, and I replied less than a second after: 'C u there.' That I didn't even ask for a time impressed her. 'Felt like we'd click.' But we didn't jump; she greeted me with the most glorious bonfires. She'd set fire to the cars parked along Triệu Thị Trinh Street, torching every single one she passed. Look at you—I get it; you find this hard to believe. I hadn't known joy could be that simple: you throw a burning rag under a car and wait for flames to burst out, crunch, distort anything they swallow. I looked at the fire and thought of nothing else; all my being focused on the entirety of its beauty from the moment of its outbreak to its extinction. That fire burned away all my grogginess after the long flight from the US and sparked an endless summer holiday.

It's been ten years. Perhaps Mi now goes under another name, like I do. Go ahead and smoke, don't be shy, you must've seen my second husband puffing on his cancer stick at the gates. He's a simple man asking simple questions: do you love me, why do you love me, do you still meet your ex these days. He never asks how many names I've gone through. Mi, every time I picked her up, she'd ask 'what should I call you today?' Madonna, Gamma, Khat Leaf, Snap, Bristle, Thorn. A new name excited us to no end, as if it was a new version of us to live out. My ex, a Japanese-born, always had problems at the airport because every holiday he would do a full-face job. A painful, not to mention costly metamorphosis, but as he used to say, 'in the end, it's great to be a new person.' That's not Mi, who always said, why so serious, it's just a game. Wolf, Rain, Anne Frank, Lolita. But I prefer to call her Mi. It was the name she claimed, walking into the police station, the last day we were together.

It was such a long time ago, and what felt like such a big deal seems pretty childish looking back now. The same way you grow up and the river in front of your childhood home is now a small brook. We toppled that monument, 'Victory', in the square. Yep, I know it's still there. They put it back right away, what do you expect, but look closely and you'll see a fine crack around the knee. No, don't bother googling it, the media all got slapped with a gag order. Do you think they'd want to let slip the truth, that the multibillion monument was pulled down easy as sneeze by two mere girls with a truck and a chain, reason being the concrete mass was reinforced with nothing but a few bamboo sticks. Like a human without a skeleton, you know how it is, all those roads and bridges and buildings being pushed up and we never know what rottenness we're living upon. We dragged it for a short distance before ditching both truck and statue, and got a room in Milky Way for a jolly night of caresses. Her skin was soft and fluffy, I always felt like I was touching cotton. I wanted to sleep after lovemaking but she said we'd better go to the police station before they grabbed us.

We were never arrested, because we always sought the police ourselves. Go ask the chief at Central Station if you want. He probably hasn't retired; I just saw him in uniform clearing the market the other day. Still chunky the way he was ten years ago, the first time I saw him I wondered how someone so lipidically-endowed could chase after criminals. At the time of our interrogation, he was just a major with a partiality for mint-flavoured cigs.

Why do I remember that, because he kept blowing smoke into my face in that claustrophobic room, those poor saturnine clouds could find no way to pass onto their next world. Separating us was a metal table sporting various dents, suggesting bleeding foreheads. Physical torture, though, is something that happens to anyone but us. As you can imagine, our family names were the invisible armour protecting me and Mi.

'Must be some organisation behind you ladies?' the chunky officer had asked me. The question made me snort. Felling a monument with such a name must've been a somewhat political act, that was their usual line of reasoning. I said every statue in this land shares the same countenance, whether holding a book, hugging a bundle of rice or wielding a sword, the icy emotionless rigidity remains the same, you can't tell them apart unless you pay very close attention. A few nights before, standing there smoking, Mi had pointed at the shadow-sword pricking my thigh and said, they should plant a tree here. 'A tree-shadow never hurts anyone,' Mi said. 'Cuz I like trees.' That was all there was to it.

I remember how I kept yawning throughout the interrogation. The officer maintained a bored façade from beginning to end, as if his questioning was just a matter of routine, a quota of pages to be filled. 'Won't come to nothing at any rate,' his attitude seemed to say. As if he knew that a few minutes later Mi's people would barge in and take her away with utmost solicitousness. They would wrap a gigantic towel around her, and offer her a water bottle and cookies, I bet you'd find it so amusing, as dramatic a scene as the ending of a disaster movie when survivors are led out of the wreckage. Passing me with a smile, Mi gestured as if asking if I wanted a drag. The woman who seemed to be her mother was touching Mi's forehead, with the back of her hand, as if her palm would be too rough and damage her daughter.

The chunky officer didn't look amused though; he pulled up his belt (forever trying to slip off his barrel of a belly) and asked his drowsy colleague: 'Sleepwalking? Again? They haven't come up with some new excuses?'

Got it? Mi was never detained because she was always innocent; her throwing rocks at lamps in the square or turning fire water hydrants to the max or blowing up a bridge pile were all done while sleepwalking. What, you want to know if it was true? Yes, according to our lawyer, and no, according to the police. When you've lived to a certain age you don't ask whether or not something is true, you ask whose truth it is. But don't you think it's just too exquisite an explanation? That with the coming of the night someone would get out of you, put on such a tattered denim jacket, and slip out through the front gates of the mansion at the end of Mỵ Nương Street, or the back gates of the Mimosa Garden, or sometimes from the villa at no. 14 Trưng Vương. That she would meet up with her friend and together go up to the Northern coach station, empty as a graveyard at this hour but for a place doing porridge and salted eggs, where they serve the crunchiest marinated cucumber you can find. Sometimes they drop by Underworld, the tapioca noodle joint, fall asleep on those ancient graves as they wait for it to open, and wake up to eyelids heavy with dew. When they drive by Mê Linh Square, a site favoured by flea markets and where summer kids would roam about, a wind or several winds convening there would suddenly toss the corpse of a kite at their speeding convertible. The kite has grown cold, but there is about it still the scent of all the sunshine it has drunk to the brim when the day was nearing its end. July is a time for night rains, they would stand forgetting time under the awning of a long-closed coffee shop, eyes drinking in the slanting tilting yellow rays of rain under the yellow lamplight, rain so willowy and silky you never notice it during the day. A chill breath blows; the girl does up her neck button and lets down her sleeves, normally rolled up; she reaches for the smooth white pebbles she always carries in her pockets (as smooth and white as her skin), the kind gardeners strew in those Chinese evergreen pots, and takes them out to throw at the houses lining the street in their slumber. Her companion figures she wants to alert those inside to her passing by, even though all she says is ' 'Cuz'. At times she would abruptly hit the brakes, jump out the door and disappear down a dark alley, then reappear a moment later looking frustrated and bewildered as usual, murmuring ' 's not here'. Her friend doesn't know what she's looking for, but has got used to her talking to herself out of nowhere, muttering 'must be inside something red', as well as to their nightly exchange of greetings, always as if for the first time. Name's Bat, yours? Mi!

Until the end, I never knew if Mi was her real name. When she got into her car surrounded by her folks, I did wonder what she'd call herself the next time we met. But that next time never came; that early morning, on their way to the police to bail me out, my parents' car was hit by a container truck. Many news outlets reported on that accident at the three-way Fog Crossroads, which left three dead. It also left my family in ruins. Even now, I still dream of waking up in my old bed to my belly rumbling and the sound of my parents fighting downstairs.

CHAPTER ELEVEN

leaving

Day two thousand and forty-six, the one who calls himself The Lord has nothing left but his heart. The woman who is to take it is crossing the river, her babe in her arms.

translator's note

It has been an honour and a challenge to translate Nguyễn Ngọc Tư, whose works enchanted her first readers not only by tales from her watery homeland but also, and foremost, by the lyrical employment of her particular flavour of Mekong Delta dialect. Remarking about the richness of Southern expressions in her early works, the diasporic professor Trần Hữu Dũng once said in a 2005 interview: 'We should just tell foreigners who wish to appreciate her works to the fullest: learn Vietnamese, you would find it a precious blessing!' Translators, of course, do not agree; translating her stories (successfully) is a dream to many practitioners of the art, including this one, and aspiring translators use one story or another from her prolific output for their personal projects.

Water: A Chronicle (first published in Vietnamese in 2020) presents a slightly different set of challenges. Now, it is less a matter of reproducing the spirit of the Southern countryside that breathes and pulses through her words, but finding a balance between the (sometimes over-) literary quality of the writing and a sense of wide-eyed artlessness, like a rural girl visiting the city for the first time. Like the Little Dragon Maidens in this book, there are layers to Nguyễn Ngọc Tư's stories: the saintly, the wicked, the void in the place of a human heart, the desire to fill that void. The mosaic novel reflects her tireless labour through the years to cast aside the stereotype of the twenty-something 'voice of the Mekong Delta' and crystallises her many explorations in various styles and genres: as journalist, essayist, poet, and chronicler both of urban hyperrealism and rural fantastic extravagance.

It is my hope that this translation reflects to a satisfying extent the range of her voice. I owe much to editor and friend Deborah Smith, whose linguistic brilliance is responsible for much of the stylistic delight that you must have appreciated, especially in rendering dialects and colloquialisms. My gratitude also goes to Khánh Nguyên, who ensured that no local cultural or linguistic nuances were missed. Lastly, I extend my thanks to Major Books and Quyên Nguyễn, for trusting and supporting this lifelong admirer from the North to adequately represent this treasure of Southern Vietnamese literature.

***

This is not the first time Nguyễn Ngọc Tư's works have been translated into English. *Cánh đồng bất tận*, the 2005 novella that first established her as the book-loving nation's darling, was translated by Dương Mạnh Hùng and Jason A. Picard as *Endless Field* (NXB Trẻ/Youth Publishing House, 2019), primarily available through Trẻ's distribution channels in Vietnam. There was also a 2012 collection titled *Floating Lives*, seemingly published in Indonesia, though details about it are scarce. And then there are the occasional short stories in various collections, mostly academic. Similar collections, nearly all containing the famous novella, also appeared in German, French, and Swedish, with the German *Endlose Felder* winning the 2018 LiBeraturpreis, awarded to female authors from the Global South. But for an author who has published nearly thirty titles by 2024, including short stories, essays, children's books, and two novels, Nguyễn Ngọc Tư remains one of Vietnamese literature's best-kept secrets.

Every new translation into a new market is an invitation, a risk, a tremble of hope. With this publication by Major Books, I hope interest would be sparked enough to pave the way for her other works, and a new audience would come to appreciate the way this unassuming author combines literary finesse with widespread appeal.

Nguyễn An Lý
Saigon, September 2024

Coming soon from Major Books

The Tale of Kiều

A new translation in verse of a national classic that has enchanted readers across generations and shaped the cultural landscape of Vietnam.—epic poem by Nguyễn Du, translated by Nguyễn Bình, first publication estimated circa 1821 (still debated)

Making a Whore

Formerly banned for over 50 years, Vũ Trọng Phụng's liberating 'exposé' is a raw and unflinching account of desire and duty in 1930s colonial Vietnam—a society stranded between influxes of Westernisation and imbedded Eastern conservative values.—novel by Vũ Trọng Phụng, translated by Đinh Ngọc Mai, first published in 1937